CITIZEN
STEELE

CITIZEN STEELE

Peter Shaindlin

DEUXMERS

Published by Deuxmers, LLC
PO Box 440, Waimanalo, Hawaii.

Cover design by Ara Feducia.

Printed in the United States of America.

ISBN: 978-0-9835041-4-6

First Edition, January 2012
Second Edition, March 2015

TO THE BERLIN GROUP

The main point is the theory of what can be expressed by propositions—i.e., by language ... and what cannot be expressed by propositions, but only shown; which, I believe, is the cardinal problem of philosophy ... what can be said at all can be said clearly, and what we cannot talk about we must pass over in silence.

— Ludwig Wittgenstein

To pretend, I actually do the thing: I have therefore only pretended to pretend.

— Jacques Derrida

PREFACE

Having received inquiries as to the true nature of this work, the principle purpose of this second edition preface is to address these topics with the hope that it will enrich the depth of the reader's experience. In the interest of fluency there is one textual alteration to the first edition: the sections composed of excerpts from Ludwig Wittgenstein's *Tractatus Logico-Philosophicus* have been reintroduced in consolidated fashion without their numerical headings.

I deplore the idea of process as a primary focal point in achieving understanding in art: it is a painful manifestation of an inability to comprehend or accept a work's inherent, tangible mysteries; "knowing" as a linear cognitive industry versus simple acceptance. Philosopher W. V. O. Quine condemned his contemporary Jacques Derrida for what he regarded as insufficient rigor in the testing of his philosophical propositions—a disturbing example of process as a qualitative measuring stick with respect to the quality of philosophical vision. An implicit related assumption is that nothing is valuable unless it is deconstructed or measurable, whereas quite often the most precious things are in fact immeasurable and resist deconstruction completely. This same type of insistence informs the curiosity of the patron pursuing an understanding of the technique of the artist more so than his vision. On a related note, Roland Barthes condemned the heavy-handedness of documentary photography through the amplification of metaphor as technique, an image's message painfully obvious due to visualized didactic condescension. Balthus bluntly discouraged the discussion of art in favor of pure contemplation, a paradigm I generally endorse. As the book's eponymous protagonist declares, "not everything can be explained."

In the case of visual arts, the viewer asks "*how?*", whereas in the case of literature, the reader asks "*why?*" To what can we attribute this distinction? The former speaks to process while the latter questions motive. It is this idea of motive that I see as critical; in addition to answering the literary question above, it speaks to the psychology of the act, a concept espousing haptic-philosophical perspectives.

The protagonist Steele withdraws from the inanity of a quotidian reality in favor of ideologies subjugated within the dark theoretical shadows of his idol, the Austrian philosopher Wittgenstein. As futility begins to permeate every aspect of his life he not only discovers the inability of philosophy to save himself, but on a more profound level that its very basis is flawed, that what with its fetid praxis it offers no real value to society. He comes to regard the discipline as stillborn, lacking animus, asphyxiated by its own hypothetical propositions. This dialectic—his unapologetic agon with Wittgenstein—not only erodes his regard for theoretical truth; it also begins to extinguish his sanity.

To step inside *Haus Wittgenstein* in Vienna, an edifice designed in great part by Wittgenstein during a period of deepening mental deterioration, is to stand within the very mind of a pronouncedly unhinged individual. In this shockingly cold and austere structure every room is like an emotional crypt in which his purported architectural and design machinations are physical extensions of his compulsive-obsessive tendencies. Is it any surprise then that in the end Steele cannot help but feel deceived and implicitly abandoned by such a coldhearted soul? In the case of him contemplating Wittgenstein, we witness a "conversation" of sorts between schizophrenics, not unlike the experience of navigating the catacombs of this chilly domicile.

To what degree is the protagonist is engaged in reality versus delusion? There is a clear distinction from a philosophical viewpoint between the ideas of existence and reality: Cartesian dogma would have us accept that we function within the realm of what exists and is destined, whereas Lockean theory denotes a bifurcation between the precepts of a reality-centered ontology of behaviors and what is ostensibly *meant* to happen. Steele disturbs our classical notion of reality through his perceptions of what he sees take place versus what others *imagine* is happening.

I would suggest that *everyone* is losing his mind: we collectively suffer this plight yet in logical discord due to the dissimilar pace and nature of individual experience. Deterioration is the very essence of the human condition, and not just physically: emotional dissolution is also a natural organic function. In traditional burial the body rots until it ceases to exist, as do our lives in terms of experiential expression of the soul. Due to society's vast composite of differing personalities it bears a "collective" schizophrenia of its own, within which exist individual schizophrenics as in the case of Richard Jason Steele.

The local authorities are not in the least bit comfortable with the fact that Steele "sees" things differently: this is sufficient reason to permanently extricate him from society so that the spirit of Nietzche's collective "numbness" may continue. As a corollary with immediacy at the onset of *The Trial*, Kafka renders irrelevant the idea of factual specificity; the accused attempts to dismiss motive by virtue of alibi but to no avail as the authorities are predisposed as to his guilt.

Notwithstanding his eventual rejection of Wittgenstein's fixation with semiotic aspects of language, Steele remains beholden to symbolism: it is not for art's sake that he adores Piero Di Cirico's painting *St. John the Evangelist*—from within it he finds salvation at the notion of adoration itself.

Here, art demonstrates greater value than philosophical ruminations. As Frederick R. Weismann once noted, "Art is quicker than language and clearer than philosophy."

Dreams and apparitions are of the same family of cossetting, mysterious reveries for Steele, his final refuge. Lawyers—the master race of faux-intelligentsia, surround him at work, not unlike the way co-workers did with Kafka in his dull and dismal Prague insurance office. In Steele's "inner world" the matter of theory exists as the basis for behavior more so than moral considerations; in order to establish ethical boundaries for himself he must first determine the essence, the material nature of existence itself. In this way, he is more attuned to the precepts of Berkeley than of Locke; of Hume than Des Cartes. Ultimately unconvinced of his very own existence, he has no choice but to abandon Wittgenstein. Exacerbating his predicament is the philosopher's use of language as a principal vehicle in the confirmation of existence. Derrida characterizes this conundrum succinctly: "In a language, in the system of language, there are only differences ... consciousness offers itself to thought only as self-presence, as the perception of self in presence." With similar realization, Steele determines that concepts like guilt and punishment have no actual power as they cannot exist in the absence of his *own* existence. In such a paradigm the mind dictates reality as opposed to nature. He is not in a cell, he is in the distant town of Arcombe with his mystical companion Moon, or in the park behind his condominium; he exists wherever he imagines he exists. Philosophy loses validity in the absence of predicaments. In one sense his journey suggests the possibility that through schizophrenia (which we regard as an affliction), the individual is liberated per se from the restrictions of sanity; he is in a void of consciousness through which his new philosophical bent negates all physical and emotional contingencies. Insanity is the most extreme case of retreat, safe harbor for the disillusioned and disenfranchised. We would assume that, being deranged, the ostensibly afflicted cannot understand this, yet Steele's view of the circumstances suggests otherwise.

I have been told that a novel cannot end in a poem, but I tend to think of novels as vast poems not unlike how Bloom characterizes Shakespeare's plays. The Eliot excerpts which I reconstructed out of sequence and further embellished with additional original lines and vocabulary were as much of an experiment as anything else. I personally find his *Four Quartets* arrhythmic and disjunctive; at any rate, reconstructed as such they suit the conclusion of the story.

A writer explaining himself after-the-fact is as pointless as a chef explaining how he set about preparing some plate of food by sequentially deconstructing the process: he chopped carrots and minced onions with celery—he explained his *mise en place*, thereby denuding a process which notwithstanding its legitimacy was but a means-to-an-end. Herein lies the problem of Wittgenstein in terms of intent: he reasonably assumed that the reader would deduce the purpose of his construct by virtue of content; the same was the case with this book and in turn the Wittgenstein excerpts I chose, given both their essence and relative juxtaposition within the novella's text. Gore Vidal was once asked, what should a group of well-educated readers do who could not clearly comprehend his book? His answer: "Read it again!" The same was the case with Faulkner: "Some people say they can't understand your writing, even after they have read it two or three times. What approach would you suggest for them?" "Read it four times."

I have attempted to facilitate that reader's second attempt, with slight compromise yet no contrition.

Peter Shaindlin
Honolulu, January 1, 2015

A number of people served directly or indirectly as inspiration for this book: Special thanks to John Chalmers, Jana Wolff, Roberta Senatore and Dr. Allana Wade Coffee for their trusted input.

I

I decided to go to a Jungian psychologist yesterday to solve some problems I was having and when I mentioned Philemon she didn't know what I was talking about. I thought, what is going on here?! I dismissed myself early from the session and paid her the one hundred dollars anyway. I went down to the street and smoked a filterless cigarette and watched a homeless woman get splashed by a city bus parting a lengthy puddle of water that got her across the chest. Rain pounded down steadily. I had a brief burst of random simultaneous thoughts that included Disraeli, Plastic Wood, paperback books and eraser dust plus a few other things I could not remember within a nanosecond. My name is Richard Jason Steele.

I have been told that I have ADHD a number of times in the past few years since it became trendy. They say it's a "disease" but I don't buy it: I always thought diseases involved viruses—some kind of bacterial thing in your blood, something communicable. But now it seems that the popular definition involves any societal, chemical or drug-induced behavior that evokes self-pity and external contempt. I had a friend for example with Epstein-Barr: he was really just a depressed, lazy misfit. When he finally, thankfully somehow got his act together the doctors claimed they had cured him through a combination of therapy and medication.

I went into a Ramen shop and sat towards the middle of the long yellow Formica countertop. Young Japanese males lined the rest of the counter in both directions. They slurped their soup even when they didn't need to. I felt conspicuously Caucasian. At first the excessive brightness of the fluorescent lighting above irritated me but that was surpassed rapidly by more slurping sounds of the patrons on either side of me. It seemed a way of fitting in, being conformative and non-threatening. That odd, ubiquitous pinkish oval pork scrap or whatever it was floated around pointlessly in my soup bowl. I picked it out and put it on my napkin using my chopsticks, which drew stares, but I didn't care. How sex could come into my mind within such an environment is rude and perhaps even appalling. I would be off of work for the next three days and had this idea that I should spend some time in the peep shows, which were cheap and mildly stimulating. I went to use the men's room and the only urinal was occupied so I pushed the door open of the single stall to determine whether the toilet was usable. Formica again came into play as I took in the filthy, graffiti-marked dusty-rose hue of the despicable waste chamber. Back in the shop I paid my bill; it came out to: $7.48.

Upon returning to the street I pulled up my collar and felt the mild sting of the brisk night air; the rain continued steadily but not too heavily. I walked several blocks and got to a dark and quiet intersection. I saw a girl maybe in her early twenties at the opposite curb looking as if she was wanting a lift someplace. She had long brown hair, a damaged Burberry umbrella and seemed passably attractive. I felt a slight sexual urge common to my gender and crossed at the light, walking purposely right by her. She glanced at me and then looked back at the oncoming cars to look busy but they were ignoring her so far. I asked her if she needed anything; she looked at me this time with a scowl. I stood still with my chilled hands in the outer bottom pockets of my pea coat. She couldn't have been more than ten feet away. She realized I had stopped to watch her and she simply went about her business, sheepishly holding up her thumb to signal her desire for a ride to wherever the hell she was going. I thought she could be a prostitute, or just a wretch or maybe simply a dumb nice naive ignorant idiot that was good-looking, or some combination of the above. With nothing to lose and no clear motivation other than sloth or boredom I asked her again with shamelessness if I could be of help. I noticed then that her Navy hose was torn right down the inside of her right leg. Her muscles seemed toned and she appeared athletic, or at least in good shape. I asked her if she wanted money and she said no. I told her I had a small hotel room available nearby that was dry and warm and she paused, looking me over carefully and then saying "OK." We began walking faster than I could figure out how to play it so I didn't say anything for a bit and neither did she. I handed her a cigarette but she refused it, waving it off with one hand while looking away expressionlessly.

We took our wet coats off once in the room; she turned and faced me. She told me that she was going someplace and needed to get there soon but in fact did need cash and that she was willing to give me ten minute's time in exchange for whatever I saw fit to offer her. The vagueness of her financial demand for some reason threw me off and suddenly diminished my sexual confidence. I thought quickly, trying to salvage something of the situation for myself. As I was doing so she crossed her arms like only girls do and swiftly pulled off her thick knit sweater and there was nothing beneath it. She stood staring at me and was suddenly lovely and breathless, or so I wanted to believe. Why, don't ask me, but just then I had visions of potatoes being chopped at a Munich Movenpick by chubby German High School girls.

II

As a large international corporation doing business in one of the world's great metropolises, Faber and Faber was certainly contributing little of value to mankind while making billions by virtue of the simple principle of selling something for somewhat more than it had paid for it. As long as you could have someone buy from you under such circumstances and feel good about it you were destined for success. So the secret was to figure out a way to present the transaction in a way that appealed to the emotional desires of the recipient. The very nature of most business activities is inherently shameless. My boss, the senior partner within our in-house legal department, was fat, older and stupid. I always held a general disdain for fat people because most of them can do something about it but choose not to. They just stuff their faces with almost anything they can get their hands on. I figure you either weigh more or less than you did yesterday and that's the end of the story, period. So it must be a manageable circumstance. What does overweight mean, anyway—over *what* weight? They're fat, that's all. And they don't seem to give a shit. I sat there in my soulless cubicle and briefly considered the events of the night before. My thoughts jumped suddenly to the psychologist again. She had several diplomas on her office wall, one from Harvard University. But she knew nothing of Jung's lakeside companion. I wanted to go back in time to the previous evening and ask the mystery girl—I don't even know what her name is—if she knew who Philemon was. Maybe she *was* Philemon. But it was too late. She had slipped back into the night without even asking for the money. I myself of the insidious and pervasive mental virus had forgotten that I even owed it to her. So it does seem I do have a condition of sorts, depending on how one might define or distinguish a condition from a disease. The fact that I was ostensibly in debt to her did disturb me somewhat. I wondered how I could have intercourse with a nameless woman, likely never see her ever again but nevertheless owe her something. The boss stuck his fat perspiring head in my open door for a moment and yelled at me to bring the Masterson file to his office post-haste. It didn't consciously register at the time he spoke—strains of Thomas Canning's *Fantasia on a Hymn* were running through my head. I looked at a plastic folder sitting all by itself in the center of my desk. It was blue, the sort of semi-artificial sky-blue that was synthetic yet pleasant in its color temperature. I gazed at it absentmindedly and the Canning strings suddenly surged through me with voluminous ecstasy; at the same time I saw blurred mathematical numbers/equations floating around the folder, inches above the desktop. Pi was prevalent and always made me feel relaxed. I felt hungry and imagined stuffing a slightly chilled glazed donut into my mouth. The file. Yes, the Masterson file. That's what I had been trying to focus on. The Masterson Trust was complex, unusual yet genuinely jejune in almost every way. The trust would automatically dissolve itself in less than two years, after some forty-eight years of longevity. There were originally some twenty-two beneficiaries but over the years various of them had died and willed their shares to either family members, business, friends of even arcane charities in God-forsaken corners of the United States of America, places as appalling as Pensacola, Florida, Jebbs, Idaho and even Lark-to, Iowa.

I wondered why I ever went to law school in the first place. It was my job as an estate attorney to advise our clients who were members of the trusts as to how to handle the renegotiation of their leases and partnerships in the face of the soon-to-expire agreement. The complexities were immense and in many ways inherently subjective in the application of a determination as to how to handle the pending transitions in the best interest of the parties in question. Such was the *ennui generale* of my employment. Generally lawyers are bores: they share an unwritten code of feigned general superiority—they equate their prior academic acumen with superior intellect, yet in doing so they obviate the abstract aspect of innate intellectual capability in favor of strategy as an enduring value. My mind drifted off once again: Charles Canning's use of the celli was far subtler than Copeland's, I pondered: Copeland was ultimately crude in a way not dissimilar to Orff in the case of Carmina

Burana—it was obvious. And the less-than-cryptic text accompanying the Burana made it all the worse for wear, I'd always thought. Even Mahler I felt achieved only crudity at best with his brass orchestrations, even by the time of his seventh symphony. In his New York Times obituary he was identified in the headline as a "celebrated conductor" who also composed. She was good last night, I decided—whoever she was. And the Burana text reminded me of her, too. "I want to know your loins, I want to know your loins; this is for you and for the heavens, what we are doing ..." And so on. I wondered what her name was. I absentmindedly began peeling a slightly under-ripe banana; my boss was barking at me now for the file. I stared up at him as he gazed at me almost in disbelief as though I was some kind of an idiot. I suddenly remembered that it was the blue file right in front of me and I handed it to him with concealed regret as I could still see the lyrical, bouncing jig of the numerals swirling about it as he took it impatiently from my hand. I imagined a three-dimensional pi symbol that smelled like lemons.

III

I walked briskly through the park at lunchtime. It was one of those balmy, bright but chilly fall afternoons where the maudlin quality of the fading sun around three-thirty or so makes one want to lie down and die in a beautiful, submissive sort of way. I thought about pot roast and the smell of shallots and my Great Aunt's perfume in church in New Jersey when I was six. I wanted to crawl on top of her and have her hold me. I had a vague memory of my father's car, a meticulously maintained turquoise Ford Falcon. I sat down on a green wooden bench and lit a cigarette; it tasted strong and good. It was set in a patch of spotty, faded thick grass with a few low-lying shrubs here and there.

I looked to my left and saw a man in a grey flannel suit lying supine with a chef's knife stuck into his chest. He was maybe early sixties, tall, with an imposing look not unlike say John Huston or Joseph Cotton. There was a small circle of dried blood around the wound where the knife had penetrated his suit. He was looking rather relaxed and timeless, actually. A diamond from his tie clip shimmered briefly in the sunlight. As he lay directly behind a shrub, I seemed to be the only one nearby who'd noticed him. The occasional passerby invoking a mid day constitutional was oblivious, again due to the close proximity of the corpse to the surrounding shrubbery. I looked straight ahead for a moment and took a long drag on the smoldering fag in my right hand. I knew I should report what I saw and so got up, turned left and made for the local precinct which I knew to be two blocks away near the main midtown intersection. I wondered what my boss would think of this?

In the end I was judged an annoyance to the detectives and officers on the scene. No body was there when we returned; sirens were employed as we raced back to the park in three squad cars, for a brief moment a melodramatic caravan en route to some heinous scene that to their disappointment never actually transpired. Their confusion and subsequent irritation over the lack of an actual corpse upon arrival there was palpable; suddenly I was treated more like a suspect than an informer. It was interesting to me that in the absence of a victim I became a person of suspicion. Eventually they warned me not to play games with their time and the peoples' resources. I received perfunctory admonitions regarding the notion that I had jeopardized other erstwhile innocent victims by deterring their energies over an apparent hoax.

I went back to my office and the rest of the afternoon was uneventful. Returning home from the local market that evening around seven with a bag of groceries I noticed a grey sedan parked across the street in an illegal zone with what appeared to be two plainclothes police officers. There was no question that they were observing me. I wondered why they would be there, but then, remembering the suspicious and untrusting nature of the Captain on the scene it struck me that they may have decided to observe me for a bit as my earlier actions had seemed quite peculiar to them. My thought at the time was that he resembled a slightly aged version of Apollinaire if he had been more worn and unhappy in appearance. As for what might have happened to the body I saw—and I *know* that I saw one—I had absolutely no idea at the time. I could only conclude that in the short time I had been at the stationhouse it had been moved. Who knows why?

I observed a bright yellow aura about their automobile and its energy seemed frenetic to me. I proceeded through the vestibule and up the stairs towards my second floor flat. The dreary hallway smelled of sticky rice and burnt garlic. It must be that goddamned old Malaysian bitch in the second floor flat, the one who fries fish every Tuesday.

IV

The next day I hopped down the stairs of the building and across the street on the way to the subway as I headed off to work. Birds on the wires above chirped incessantly against an aural backdrop of accelerating buses, car horns and scratchy AM radio talk shows from somewhere off in the distance. I skipped down the stairs to the train station, scanned my monthly card and hopped into the closest crowded car just as the doors were closing. Who was I pressed right up against but the woman from two nights earlier?

She looked me right in the eye and quietly yet firmly demanded her money. I fumbled, reached into my wallet trying not to be obvious and discreetly handed her a fifty-dollar bill. She slipped it into her coat pocket, said nothing and then stared straight down at the floor of the train car. The train continued on from station to station and she never moved a bit, looking the whole time like a De Lempicka subject in timeless repose. I got out at my stop and left her standing there; she not once looked up at me or said a word. The experience was disturbing for sure but then I thought, oh, I'm lucky; she didn't get crazy or lay a trip on me.

The meeting regarding the Masterson Trust ran on all day; what a bore. The agreement itself was stupid and so were both my clients and the trust board. What was the point of such affairs? Why did I give my career, my life to this? I left the office for home at around six-thirty and the wind really picked up. It was cold as hell and all I wanted was a stiff shot of bourbon in the solitude of my apartment. Silence. That was all. After two generous drinks I walked up the remaining three flights to the roof and braced myself in the cold night air as the erratic gusts laced over the top of the building and rattled the television antennae haphazardly placed about the tarry, uneven grey surfacing. I was in one of my periodic catatonic moods and so I took up my normal position on the southeast corner standing right up on the foot-high corner brace to look down five floors above the sprawling, glittering metropolis below. I watched various near and far light sequences of green, yellow and red play off each other at random semaphores as cars succumbed to their dull luminosities. Nobody along the street below ever seemed to take notice of me. Pondering what might happen to the Masterson Trust situation if I were to perish suddenly, I determined that my loss would be inconsequential in the end to all those involved. Perry, a senior partner with great dislike for me would take things over until they were resolved and receive an even larger bonus at year-end than already likely. So why give him the satisfaction, I thought? With that, I stepped back off the outer ledge and lit another cigarette.

V

When I got to my office building the next morning I was delayed from entering for a good fifteen minutes or so as a woman had jumped to her death from the eighteenth floor, according to coworkers I encountered behind the police lines. Rumor had it she had found her husband cheating on her with his secretary late the previous night in his office. I wondered if he would discontinue the affair permanently given the circumstances and decided it was highly unlikely. I must admit I was rather shocked at myself for having been irritated at the woman in question for causing me delay in getting to my workplace, but that's how I felt.

When I had left my building that morning the same car was across the street with one of the same two men in it; the other I had seen in the park during the investigation there and I assumed him to be another detective. When I returned home that night they were standing together at the steps of my building having a smoke. They showed their badges and asked if they could speak to me upstairs. I offered them bourbon and they accepted, contradicting policy, which was a bit surprising to me as they knew I was a lawyer. They asked me a variety of questions, pretty much the same ones they had asked three days ago on the Monday when I had first discovered the corpse. So I gave the same answers. They seemed dissatisfied and we all then lit cigarettes without a word being spoken. They were surprised I allowed smoking within my apartment—the shorter, fatter one named Mullen remarked that no one smokes at home any more. I told them look, I saw what I saw and was simply trying to do the right thing. That they said was what made them suspicious in the first place. Another long silence while we all reflected on whatever that might mean. Mullen looked down at a copy of *The Magic Mountain* by Thomas Mann on my coffee table and asked if it was a travel book. Of sorts, I answered. Again, an awkward, idiotic pause where they said nothing.

They decided we should all walk back together to the park to look around. Of course there was nothing there but still they had me reenact my whereabouts and discovery of the body. They eventually parted unceremoniously and I sat back down on the bench for one last smoke before retiring for the evening. This time there were virtually no passers-by; a smudgy grey sky succumbed to darkness and of course at that later hour the park was empty of people as well. I turned to my left and observed the Hawthorn bush where I had seen the body, its small, brittle leaves shaking in minute, tremulous unison against the frigid zephyrs of winter wind.

Not too much later on that evening I leaned over the coffee table in my small dark living room and thumbed through the first chapter of *Tractatus Logico-Philosophicus* by Ludwig Wittgenstein, the brash Austrian philosopher whose thinking had for years permeated the very essence of myself, ethically and morally. My particular edition of the celebrated philosophical tome was small, linen-bound and worn on all of its fading, dingy edges. Ironically, it had been given to me by my father, a person who himself had never once uttered a single contemplative word to me. It was the type of book that required a certain tactile sensitivity on the part of the reader as its inner binding, dry and fragile at the hands of time periodically gave way to one's fingertips that, upon turning a page with distracted enthusiasm would all too often provoke a *petit mort* as it suddenly tore free of the threads that had governed its proper place amongst its hundreds of identical companions.

As always, it sucked me in, never being able to read just one individual sentence at a time—each subsequent one was like a kind of confusing yet titillating addiction.

He began aggressively from the get-go with his hard-boiled deconstruction of philosophical entities; he was so bold to have inferred to Russell that with this work he could and would inarguably "resolve" the matter of philosophy itself: whereas certain of his predecessors had discovered the philosophic atom, he intended to split it. Perhaps no philosopher before him had been so blunt and emphatic:

The world is all that is the case. The world is the totality of facts, not of things. The world is determined by the facts, and by their being all the facts. For the totality of facts determines what is the case, and also whatever is not the case. The facts in logical space are the world. The world divides into facts. Each item can be the case or not the case while everything else remains the same. What is the case—a fact—is the existence of states of affairs. A state of affairs (a state of things) is a combination of objects (things). It is essential to things that they should be possible constituents of states of affairs.

In logic nothing is accidental: if a thing can occur in a state of affairs, the possibility of the state of affairs must be written into the thing itself. It would seem to be a sort of accident, if it turned out that a situation would fit a thing that could already exist entirely on its own. If things can occur in states of affairs, this possibility must be in them from the beginning. (Nothing in the province of logic can be merely possible. Logic deals with every possibility and all possibilities are its facts.) Just as we are quite unable to imagine spatial objects outside space or temporal objects outside time, so too there is no object that we can imagine excluded from the possibility of combining with others. If I can imagine objects combined in states of affairs, I cannot imagine them excluded from the possibility of such combinations.

Things are independent in so far as they can occur in all possible situations, but this form of independence is a form of connexion with states of affairs, a form of dependence. If I know an object I also know all its possible occurrences in states of affairs. (Every one of these possibilities must be part of the nature of the object.) A new possibility cannot be discovered later. If I am to know an object, thought I need not know its external properties, I must know all its internal properties. If all objects are given, then at the same time all possible states of affairs are also given.

Each thing is, as it were, in a space of possible states of affairs. This space I can imagine empty, but I cannot imagine the thing without the space. A spatial object must be situated in infinite space. (A spatial point is an argument-place.) A speck in the visual field, thought it need not be red, must have some colour: it is, so to speak, surrounded by colour-space. Notes must have some pitch, objects of the sense of touch some degree of hardness, and so on. Objects contain the possibility of all situations. The possibility of its occurring in states of affairs is the form of an object. Objects are simple.

Every statement about complexes can be resolved into a statement about their constituents and into the propositions that describe the complexes completely.

Objects make up the substance of the world. That is why they cannot be composite. If they world had no substance, then whether a proposition had sense would depend on whether another proposition was true. In that case we could not sketch any picture of the world. It is obvious that an imagined world, however difference it may be from the real one, must have something—a form—in common with it.

Objects are just what constitute this unalterable form. The substance of the world can only determine a form, and not any material properties. For it is only by means of propositions that material properties are represented—only by the configuration of objects that they are produced. In a manner of speaking, objects are colourless.

If two objects have the same logical form, the only distinction between them, apart from their external properties, is that they are different. Either a thing has properties that nothing else has, in which case we can immediately use a description to distinguish it from the others and refer to it; or, on the other hand, there are several things that have the whole set of their properties in common, in which case it is quite impossible to indicate one of them. For it there is nothing to distinguish a thing, I cannot distinguish it, since otherwise it would be distinguished after all.

The substance is what subsists independently of what is the case. It is form and content. Space, time, colour (being coloured) are forms of objects. There must be objects, if the world is to have unalterable form. Objects, the unalterable, and the subsistent are one and the same. Objects are what is unalterable and subsistent; their configuration is what is *changing and unstable. The configuration of objects produces states of affairs. In a state of affairs objects fit into one another like the links of a chain.*

In a state of affairs objects stand in a determinate relation to one another. The determinate way in which objects are connected in a state of affairs is the structure of the state of affairs. Form is the possibility of structure. The structure of a fact consists of the structures of states of affairs. The totality of existing states of affairs is the world. The totality of existing states of affairs also determines which states of affairs do not exist. The existence and non-existence of states of affairs is reality. (We call the existence of states of affairs a positive fact, and their non-existence a negative fact.) States of affairs are independent of one another. From the existence or non-existence of one state of affairs it is impossible to infer the existence or non-existence of another. The sum-total of reality is the world.

We picture facts to ourselves. A picture presents a situation in logical space, the existence and non-existence of states of affairs. A picture is a model of reality. In a picture objects have the elements of the picture corresponding to them. In a picture the elements of the picture are the representatives of objects. What constitutes a picture is that its elements are related to one another in a determinate way. A picture is a fact. The fact that the elements of a picture are related to one another in a determinate way represents that things are related to one another in the same way. Let us call this connexion of its elements the structure of the picture, and let us call the possibility of this structure the pictorial form of the picture. Pictorial form is the possibility that things are related to one another in the same way as the elements of the picture. That is how a picture is attached to reality; it reaches right out to it. It is laid against reality like a measure. Only the end-points of the graduating lines actually touch the object that is to be measured. So a picture, conceived in this way, also includes the pictorial relationship, which makes it into a picture. These correlations are, as it were, the feelers of the picture's elements, with which the picture touches reality.

Russell, particularly in the context of his famed paradox, developed and employed his "naïve set theory" in a way that might by its very nature contradict Wittgenstein's ideas about picture theory at least to the extent that strictly speaking, the paradox threatened to negate the *universality* of pictures, or better put, *a* picture; *any* given picture. That is to say that if one assumes the mantle of the proposed paradoxical aspect in that a group represented by x cannot stand for a collection of all groups if x itself is not a member of the group but only represents all groups, then a picture, which is obviously one of a theoretical set of all pictures (equally plausible to identify as having the core characteristics of x), cannot have another different picture that represents *all* pictures yet stands alone by virtue of bearing its own unique and different characteristics, as no two images are the same. Now, even if we were to make copies of all of the same of one single picture to eliminate that problem and by doing so disprove the prior notion since other, different pictures do exist, the inescapable conclusion has to be that picture theory contradicts Russell's paradox due to the undeniable idea/fact of no two pictures being the same. That said, it seems to me that in developing his theory it is flawed specifically because Russell inadvertently ignored the question of sameness.

VI

The following night there was no surveillance car outside the building and I walked over the two blocks to the park again and stared at the bushes where I was sure the body had been. For some odd reason I felt suddenly fulfilled. I returned home and before retiring turned on the television briefly. The film *Sunset Boulevard* was playing and as the butler pushed closed the front door of an estate house he muttered to an inquisitive visitor, "I'm sorry, we have no information."

The next morning I saw a man at a breakfast kiosk that looked remarkably like the victim in the park from Monday—I was frankly astonished at his appearance. Even his suit looked distinctly like the one of the bloodied corpse on the lawn. Expressionless, he disappeared quickly enough into a crowd of commuting pedestrians along the rainy avenue.

VII

The boss was not happy, not in the least. The Masterson Trust was at peril due to the new risk of partition suit by a disgruntled member. In simple terms, this meant that *any* member of the trust—even with the most minute share—could petition a judge to force a break-up of the trust in order to address his concerns over the continued ownership of a portion of real estate that he was not convinced was in his own best interests. It could easily then end up a matter for public auction. The idea of the law was to provide an opt-out for even a minute minority owner dissatisfied with the use of the land. Since law school, this law never made sense to me, or at best it was inherently imperfect as it could simply be used to coax a profit taking situation rather than only an altruistic remedy of sorts. The boss demanded to know of me what I was going to do to prevent it and I advised him to offer to buy out the antagonist before the situation got out of hand. He summarily ignored me and then proceeded to warn me that my hopes for partnership would be effectively doused if no more viable a solution were affected by me within the next sixty days when the trust would expire. I had no other good ideas and I didn't even really know the first thing about the party in question—not even where they resided. Nevertheless, it appeared that an avaricious, otherwise inconsequential nobody maybe three thousand miles away was suddenly putting my entire career at risk of failure. I fantasized briefly about hunting him down and killing him.

But the point of least resistance for me that night was to go back up to the roof and let my feet wrap the edge of the cornerstone over the dreary street below.

VIII

I sat and returned to my computer to begin editing the first section of a work that had already tortured me for eighteen months. I became increasingly at odds with Wittgenstein's arithmetical approach towards philosophy and was disturbed by its key arguments that I viewed as myopic and ingrown, narrow by their very nature. In response I developed an idea I referred to initially as "psychological density." I needed to be able to explain this idea before attempting to deconstruct Tractatus directly as it spoke to the very nature of where I thought Wittgenstein was off the mark to begin with.

Tractatus Rejected

Prelude

I. The Inexplicable Architecture of Psychological Density

Not everything can be explained. There is thought and so there is reason, and so there is hope but inevitably, despair. But as thought is non-atomic and therefore devoid of any concrete manifested pathological virtue, its ability to affect society is only through behavior.

Psychological density speaks of the extent to which a fully developed human mind can introspectively expand upon its own natural and developed limitations in the face of the limiting aspects of non-atomic energies presented in the form of thoughts. Psychological density, being as it is affected by human thought yet un-purposefully affected and violated by primal conditioning by the parent, functions as a freestanding gubernatorial filter and modifier by which the emotional energy of the individual is insidiously curbed—in certain cases at the expense of mankind and society. This "density" is non-material and therefore non-atomic but nevertheless conjoins with the natural and inalterable energy limitations of the individual, which create a ceiling with respect to exponentiality (as apposed to emotional potency). Non-feeling thinking is not necessarily the provenance of the lesser mind, just as thinking with feeling (not unlike non-thinking while strictly feeling) does not necessarily imply ignorance or limited natural faculties. Yet in the presence of genuinely brilliant thought, feeling is dispensable at least to the extent that the logical validation of a given theorem is not diminished or negated in almost any instance by the absence of emotion within the activity scope of logical thought.

Psychological density is not evenly divisible precisely because while it appears fixed in scope and range it is in fact constantly wavering in the manner of a pulsation and so there is the real possibility that the same matter or problem put to a different mind will yield slightly different reactions each time posed even within extremely short periods of intermittence. This may also be affected in various ways by the particular time at which the matter is raised in relation to the recipient's preoccupation of the moment. *(Its indivisibility may be represented by π in terms of a constant.)* As such, logic and rationality are crippled and subjugated to incomprehensibly complex variations of atomic cerebral imperfection even before emotion perverts the quality and consistency of the process. Subjectivity is the end result.

Emotion can and does still rule and often trumps the ability of the individual to react in ways based on prevailing and conditioned morals that society would prefer. In this sense emotion is a valuable safety mechanism that disallows the external advance thoughts of others to govern and limit the behavior of the receiving individual. Sartre viewed this as a *"refuge in which we can escape to escape anguish."* *(In one sense, this might explain the rejection versus the absence per se of emotion on the part of an attorney when he pontificates, notwithstanding the propensity of such a professional to ramble more so actually because he enjoys hearing himself speak rather than that he has a point to make.)*

Even though an implied or intended thought not subsequently expressed is a real thought, it serves no purpose and holds no value per se if not linguistically communicated. Wittgenstein understood this and in this regard the significance and relationship of language to philosophy is legitimate. However, as such, language is still strictly a functional tool and only expressive in that it expresses something, yet in the end it can never express itself. Language can express the sublime but it in of itself is not consistently sublime for it is inconsistent, which confirms in one way its pluralism versus say an inanimate object—or in rarer *cases, an inanimate idea. Language in simple terms is no more than a way to get things, less frequently to bestow things. Neither of these efforts relate harmoniously with the idea of philosophy.*

An inanimate idea would be the perfect expression of infinity as a conscious state of mind, or more succinctly put, a parallax portal by which one could stop living momentarily in organic terms, perhaps long enough to exchange ideas with God.

It is possible to hypothesize that in such extreme yet magnificently rude conditions one could function otherwise normally but with an absence of "good" or "bad" we do not become unhinged in life because of good or bad ideas, acts or circumstances. Rather, we cannot manage to apply constructive logic to certain given circumstances and so we elect to brand them positively or negatively, which in turn provides us a false yet actionable basis upon which to react protectively while denying the opportunity of celebrating what is ultimately uncontrollable. We do not wish to celebrate the powerless aspects of our lives. Language is both borne of and limited by emotion, which is ultimately more expressive and extensive than words themselves.

I gazed up at the small, faded image of Wittgenstein in its humble wooden frame directly above my desk on the otherwise bare wall.

IX

While reading the morning paper several days later I saw a picture of the woman I had met on the street that night two weeks earlier. Her name was Penelope Furr and she was mentioned several times in an article in the arts section within the context of a play review. Probably her name was fake, as they all are with actors. The piece was written by an elderly columnist named Ben Wood and was entitled "Woodcraft." I gazed at her photograph. She looked to me much like Ayn Rand but prettier than her, although not as distinguished in presence as say Sylvia Plath or more so, Edna St. Vincent Millay. Her nose was long, smooth and demure, vertically pitched, narrow. The eyes were so like actresses' in that in their headshots, when they look up and off to the left, you can tell they're not really looking at anything, but rather, thinking about nothing but themselves.

It seemed strange to me that actors—always feigning their search for the "truth"—must wrap themselves in lies to present themselves. Dr. Johnson put it well when he said that anyone can stuff a pillow up their back, lunge around spasmodically and come off successfully as Quasimodo. As such none of them impressed me.

It was apparently a new minor production of Sartre's *Le Diable et le Bon Dieu* that she was appearing in. It was always hard for me to imagine Sartre wanting to construct a play as the medium naturally limits or at least controls to a great extent the nature of thought; that is to say, a play lacks any real spontaneity other than at the time of its creation, and perhaps also in the embellishments by the actors, as inherently restrictive as those may be. Anyway, it worked for Beckett, in fact brilliantly for the purpose of expressing philosophy through the medium of human behavior and implicit metaphor.

I began to wonder just what she was doing that night on the road in the rain in the first place. At that point it came over me that I met her catty-corner across the street from where I had seen the body in the park. That was strange too, but what could one really make of it at all?

I tried to relax that evening at a sidewalk café by reading Sartre—but life is naturally depressing enough without him; I could have saved myself ten dollars and felt happier. This was sheer coincidence; my interest in this book had nothing whatsoever to do with the play that Furr was in. I tossed *The Words* back on the table. Imagine the autobiography of only the first ten years of a person's life. The existentialists: look at them all; by writing all those books they only succeeded in making millions miserable along with themselves. As it happened my waitress claimed to be a literary type and so I recounted a joke concerning Sartre as she looked me up and down, coffee pot in one hand, slowly chewing gum and staring at me blankly: Sartre sat down in a Paris café one morning and asked for a cup of coffee but with no cream. His waitress responded, " … I'm sorry Monsieur Sartre, we're out of cream. We have milk though; would you like it without *milk*?" She stared a bit longer, turned on her heel and walked away.

I scanned the headline of the local newspaper: "Tot Beheaded in Luxury Building." I couldn't understand why the beheading of a child in a *luxury* building might have particular significance. On page two there was note of a ceremony concerning a milestone anniversary of the bombing of Pearl Harbor. The article was accompanied by a photograph of kamikaze pilots saluting their Japanese admiral on deck just before the mission. I wondered why they were wearing helmets.

I decided I needed to do something different and stimulating that evening: it was a Friday night and I couldn't bear the thought of another consecutive evening in the dull and listless environment that was my residence. I changed into a wool winter suit and made off for the theatre district.

Penelope Furr left me with no profound impressions from her performance that night. The play seemed as depressing as ever and I had trouble concentrating on the story, the players and even getting into a state of mind where I could gain anything whatsoever from the production itself. I imagined Shaw enduring endless versions of Wagner operas, at times restless, panicked to escape the entire often-monotonous affair. A middle-aged couple sat directly in front of me in our box and the woman would periodically glance over at her husband to her left who did the same in return. She was the typical highbrow South African Germanic female that, what with her overt adornment of pronounced diamond jewelry, accent and chiseled Teutonic features brought thoughts to mind of Eva Braun or Leni Riefenstahl.

I wondered for a moment if Wittgenstein would have found her attractive. She would offer her husband a little smile and he returned the favor but there was no way to tell if the exchange was heartfelt or perfunctory. She wore Shalimar and it made me think of churches, flower markets and the Russian Tea Room in New York. In the end they made me feel insecure and intrusive.

After the performance I slipped out quickly into the cold rainy evening and walked briskly around the corner to escape the crowd. Headed down the sidewalk past the stage door I spotted a distant neon marquis indicating an Irish pub for which I made my way.

On a recent visit there after ten o'clock I was sure I observed my boss's wife in a back booth with a gentleman I recognized but could not exactly place. He was distinguished but depressing, much like a Swiss insurance executive one might encounter at a wedding of a friend of a friend. They had a bottle of Champagne in a wine stand beside the round, banquette table; he leaned conspicuously toward her while she sat upright, feigning an innocent comportment which neither convinced nor impressed her host in the least. I don't think she noticed me. Admittedly, my sordid mind almost immediately began to imagine what type of extortive opportunity the situation might offer me in a future pinch with the firm.

Suddenly I noticed Furr exiting the establishment in the company of several people, two women and a much younger man. They exchanged pleasantries with several familiar friends or patrons at the bar as they left and the door closed behind them as they turned left towards the nearby park by foot. I thought briefly and then for no explicable reason stood and made for the entrance, heading up the avenue in the same direction but keeping a slight distance in the interest of discretion.

X

Once home I poured myself a bourbon and continued on with my thesis of sorts, in this case expanding upon the idea of our general societal inability to acknowledge the value of powerless circumstances—particularly with respect to frivolities of the human mind:

We have abandoned the value of forgetfulness. Instead we insist upon remembering; remembering everything possible. We regularly seize upon this cerebral attic of information with the intent of making "educated" decisions in the futile interest of self-protection. Moral codes are not created and enforced because they bear noble or beneficent qualities—they are introduced as fearful reactions to threats to our physical and psychological well being. Again, it appears we must protect ourselves from life, for we have already established that we cannot protect ourselves from death. Assuming that death will cause life to cease eternally, if we eliminate as much as possible the untold unpleasantries of life we cannot be happy because without those, nothing can be "pleasant" in the absence of a logically-contrasting concurrent condition.

Wittgenstein stated that death is not part of life precisely because it occurs after life. I suggest that the process or experience of dying does occur during life, and therefore, in the same way that any process is naturally connected to its end result, the experience of dying (whatever it may consist of) is also connected directly to death; as such it is arguable that certain aspects of death as an experience may be experienced by the living: there is a singular definable nanosecond that represents a bond between these two states.

As we can only hope to protect ourselves at best for the period in which we are living, we cannot protect ourselves from death. A valuable question would be, can death protect itself against us? It appears not: we consistently violate its sanctity and mystery with no clear purpose and immeasurable regret. Death is the one spectacular constant in life. It would appear for one that death as an energy force is not altered by the volume upon which it is consumed by humans and virtually all other species. Whether a single soul or an entire metropolis realizes its mortality at one time, death does not appear to alter or reveal itself as a singular or penetrable condition; it is the ultimate constant. It is not that we do not know anything certain about death; it is that we never will. Death is the mother; the universe is home.

XI

The next morning the receptionist mentioned to me upon my arrival that the boss would be in late—he had to accompany his spouse to the dermatologist. Perhaps she had a rash or some other unpleasant condition—maybe it was spread across her massive behind; at any rate I was one for which it took little to arouse my schadenfreude and so it was the case this time. I wasted no time setting my trusty little chess board atop my desk, closing the door and working out combinations of the Spanish Opening (*Ruy Lopez*) from white's perspective. By the fourth move of the classic approach to the opening the a7 pawn boldly challenges white's forward bishop and the most popular response by white is a repeated (if interim) retreat back to the second row. I wondered how at least two tempi can be lost and still white has at least equal theoretical footing to proceed and continue its attack? I froze in contemplation when suddenly my boss's ugly head appeared in my open office door. He complained about morning traffic on his sunrise commute over some bleak, endless highway and then criticized the competence of the dermatologist's receptionist. He chuckled, noting that in any case every mile took him further from his spouse. I sat still and expressionless, unable to muster any false jocular response. Little did he know of her carousing in that back booth of the Irish pub while he was likely at home in Plainville inhaling chocolate-dipped pretzels out of a bag while his dog watched in silence. After several minutes he was gone, but not before insisting that I join a small dinner party at their home the following Thursday night. Soon enough I was back to my philosophical wanderings, composing my first direct attack on Wittgenstein's opening of *Tractatus*.

II. VERE FORSIT (First Draft)

Wittgenstein's realizations regarding the core of philosophical problems were legitimately significant.

Wittgenstein identified language as a key inherent obstacle to the accurate success of philosophy as expressed in thoughts represented subsequently by language.

Languages inherently fall short of consistent universality due to each one's unique idiosyncrasies and imperfections, as Wittgenstein pointed out.

Philosophical propositions are not "facts", but are in fact alleged "truths." (Propositions cannot be facts as they cannot be substantiated by corroborative information; therefore at best they are "truths," and then only to he who wishes to believe them, regardless of his motive.)

Even in the case of a perfect or near-perfect idea, it cannot ultimately be expressed perfectly or accurately due to the imperfections of every language, which whether by oral, written or other form cannot be conveyed with adequate accuracy to a level where the "truth" of the idea may be communicated as originally intended. (Agree here with LW.)

If we assume that the imperfections of language will always naturally corrupt or pervert a given thought, than every thought expressed through language must therefore be inherently corrupt and perverted, so then every philosophical thought must be misrepresented in and of itself—ironically due at least in part to the failure of language in terms of accurate or sufficient expression.

Wittgenstein was largely concerned with the damage to thought incurred during its conversion process from thought into language. He proposed that this unavoidable failure was the key problem of philosophy and that that is what needed to be solved in order to allow for the accurate expression of philosophical thought.

Wittgenstein became preoccupied with the idea of the language conversion issue as being the primary problem of philosophy, vis-à-vis expression and accuracy of that expression and also its related and inherent limitations.

Any language is already naturally limited in its ability to match the potentially infinitesimal range of human thought and each thought's infinite possibilities of variation.

The Chinese Room Paradox confirms that Wittgenstein was incorrect in suggesting that language is the key obstacle to philosophical expression, precisely because the paradoxical situation confirms that an accurate expression of the meaning of the language was not dependent upon the user's ability to actually understand the language in order to achieve his objective. That is to say, his given thought could be expressed by virtue of "matching" language, but admittedly only to the extent that the language is capable of successfully functioning as a vehicle to express his thought. (In this regard I concede that Wittgenstein was correct in his supposition regarding the idea of difficulties existing in terms of language's capability of always being able to express philosophical expression; however, my first point in identifying the idea of "psychological density" was to confirm the idea that before the matter of language's expressive limitations can be assessed it must first be recognized that the natural limit of the given person's thought capability has an inextricable and immeasurable relationship to the language matter from the perspective of cause and effect—this much is obvious.)

The linguistic expression of philosophical thought is a secondary or "functional" aspect relative to the sharing of ideas.

A more vital and primary issue of "philosophical conversion" is actually that of "practical" or "useful" conversion. This involves the idea that philosophy only has a value if and when it is functionally applied to the individual being and/or society in general.

Only in rare instances have philosophical propositions had a direct and fairly immediate impact on societies and individuals.

Such a case would be as with Rousseau and "The Social Contract" where the masses directly received, consumed and reacted in significant ways to his ideas which in turn changed society and the human condition.

This is highly unusual; in most cases philosophy is consumed and contemplated by a select, educated few; only rarely is it seized upon in ways which actually alter the world we live in.

If i equals ideation and pl equals public limitation, then

$$\frac{i}{pl} = 0$$

Because of the public's general disinterest in and inability to process and utilize most philosophical offerings, most philosophical output remains unutilized and therefore valueless—if or until it ever is.

Most philosophy is treated abstractly for the general purpose of private enrichment and contemplation and is rarely employed by individuals in position of power to affect its ideas in practical ways which might benefit individuals or the public overall. (This is the single greatest crisis of philosophy and always has been.) This is a priori to Wittgenstein's fundamental notion that language plays a constant imbedded role within the DNA of philosophy.

Only by means of a "public filter" or interpreter will potentially valuable philosophical ideas stand a chance of being utilized for the betterment of the individual and/or society.

Such a person is often a sovereign or political leader.

Such a person must be able to accurately comprehend the given philosophical idea in question regardless of linguistic conversion challenges (such as identified by Wittgenstein).

Such a person must be able to distill its fundamental value into terms—and language—which can ultimately be comprehended by the masses without losing its core essence and message.

It is not necessary for leaders to use their own ideas, nor philosophical ideas, in order to impact society.

Philosophical ideas are not, and cannot be owned; they are only generated.

Once generated any such ideas become the permanent provenance of all societies—or, at least, inevitably.

Over time every philosophical idea will become corrupted and increasingly misunderstood.

A philosophical statement is not "a fact" as Wittgenstein proposed; it is a proposition put forth as a "newly-identified truth" with the conviction of the given philosopher in question the sole professor of the "truth."

No one philosophical proposition can hope to function purely, as countless combinations of such propositions may be combined and modified and exist at minimum by sheer inference or implication, even devoid of declaration.

The combining and/or modification of philosophical propositions does not necessarily dictate their dilution; but it is impossible to guarantee that any two or more positive propositions in and of themselves will have a positive outcome if combined in implementation.

In the absence of practical implementation all philosophical propositions are without current value. Therefore all philosophers are without value if and until the time that their ideas are employed in society in a real and meaningful way.

Philosophers need not be direct leaders, but if their ideas are utilized to benefit society then they are our de facto true leaders.

If n is the negative result representing failure for a philosophical proposition to benefit society via practical application, then

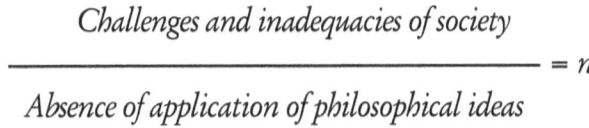

$$\frac{\text{Challenges and inadequacies of society}}{\text{Absence of application of philosophical ideas}} = n$$

That much was obvious. I looked up at Wittgenstein's picture on my wall and this time wondered, *was he a schnitzel eater?*

XII

On the way home from work that afternoon I happened by a charming little wine shop and wandered in to browse, thinking that perhaps I should buy a bottle to bring to the boss's dinner party later in the week. I immediately spotted a bottle of Echezeaux and contemplated its Napoleonic grandeur, its history, its voluptuous body. I did not wish to discuss it with the salesman standing nearby and looking me over with condescension; they always wanted to talk about "hints" and "notes." Almost without thinking I took it to the counter and immediately felt that inescapable gaze of the pathetic clerk whenever one purchased an expensive selection—you never were quite sure whether their almost smug smile was in appreciation of your taste and capability or simply their inability to conceal their envy and even perhaps greed at the specter of a significant sale. I scowled overtly as our eyes met and then exited quickly, grabbing the bagged item off the countertop and striding rapidly out towards the fresh air. My next thought was that I really didn't want to waste it on my boss, his fat disgusting wife or whomever their insipid, dull friends would end up being that night—although I did wonder if the man I thought I'd seen his wife with in the pub that night might be there.

XIII

From the get-go I found Detective Mullen an incredibly irritating person. He never quite looked me in the eye, but each time he dropped an innuendo or a rhetorical question he would slowly turn his head away from me and then look for a confirming grin from his partner Benz, purposely excluding me in effect from my own inquisition. I could not stop wondering about him each day: what motivated him, how a person like this might live. It was easy enough to locate his home address through the usual available channels; he was in a bland middle-class neighborhood within the city limits yet far enough and green enough to feel suburban. I estimated that it was within five walking blocks from the express train station.

I decided to pay my first visit to his home on a Tuesday because I remembered he had told me he was off on Sundays and Mondays. I simply wandered out of my office mid-morning following yet another dull meeting with the boss and some underlings on the case and strolled to the mid-town station. As I'd quietly traversed the long, narrow central corridor of our office suite I turned my head to and fro gazing with neutral expression at each of the series of small conference rooms whose blasé occupants were revealed to me through the rectangular glass partitions providing them conversational privacy. The unattractive, puppet-like heads of my various colleagues bobbed about, their lips moving in the type of conversation that lawyers enjoy, always the subtlest smirk on their face as they proffered some atavistic comportment that made them to feel smarter than those around them.

It was only about a fifteen-minute train ride and it was easy enough to find the house along a short block lined with almost identical little structures lacking any real character or charm. It was a single-level home; no one was to be seen on the street in either direction. I heard soft kitchen noises from within to my left. I ever so gently turned the doorknob and alas it was open. Ironic, I mused, that a detective's home would be unlocked—but then, that spoke to the arrogance that Mullen gave off whenever I'd seen him.

A faint smell of sautéed onions and chicken livers filled the air—or was it beef-based gravy? At any rate, it made me feel relaxed, even a bit drowsy. I could hear who must be his wife fiddling about in the kitchen, bright lights on in there as opposed to the dingy, depressing little living room to my right. I chose a large comfortable old dark brown leather sofa and sat down slowly, facing the television that was on at low volume with an infomercial running about some kind of "miracle" rug sweeper. Changing the channel with the remote control I happened upon *A Day at the Races* with the Marx Brothers. During a scene without dialogue in which Groucho

Marx repeatedly fumbles with a stack of books, dropping them all over the floor time and again, I was captivated by the polyrhythmic effect elicited by the sound of the falling tomes in conjunction with the clattering of pots and pans in the kitchen that Mrs. Mullen was creating. I sat for what must have been a good twenty minutes thinking about what it must feel like to be detective Robert Mullen, relaxing here, wife in the kitchen preparing dinner, cosseted by the genuine and reliable ennui of this innocuous and inconsequential neighborhood. Busy being bored. All this time she never came into the room and I never once thought about what I would have done if she had. Eventually I got up and left just as quietly and calmly as I had arrived. The train back into town was again painless and smooth and I was back at my desk unnoticed within about ninety minutes. There was a message to call Mullen or Benz. I stared at the message slip, paused and then tossed it in the empty trashcan, returning to concentrate on my work.

XIV

Every man is a failure and most are cowards as well. But those free of cowardice change thought and therefore, culture. They leave their mark in steel and their voice across the heavens in blazes of energy and light. As all men are to some extent cowardly, however, the true definition of a hero is a man who *confesses* his cowardice. This is the first and last act of truth. There are no falsehoods—they are indefinable; the idea of falseness is but an insidious expression of fear. There are only truths and as such they do not require an opposite in order to exist.

The next day Mullen kept calling and leaving messages. Not wanting to look suspicious I finally called him back. He told me they had not been able to turn anything else up on the body I had originally reported. He told me that if I had anything else to share with them I should do so post haste "in the interest of justice and self-preservation." Then he asked me something that made my hair stand on end. He wanted to know if I knew one Penelope Furr. Before even thinking, for whatever reason I told him I did not. There was an extremely long silence on the line and then without any more words he simply hung up. I sat for a brief period of time with the receiver in my hand, trying to sort out just what was going on.

I needed bourbon. I had three that night at home and then somehow suddenly found myself teetering on the corner of the roof once again. It was the very edge of darkness, the sky a wash of gunmetal hues, a nip in the air and a moderate breeze. I must have looked like a figure in a Magritte painting what with my grey flannel suit, bowler hat and silver tie clip. With my eyes closed, drink in one hand and the other extended for balance I experienced an entirely new apparition. I was standing barefoot and half-naked, lashed with leather straps to the mast of an old sailing ship. The vessel was slowly navigating rugged chop around the point of some remote uninhabited tropical island. I was bound and had been violated in some offensive way; I was a woman. I had thick, shaggy black hair, long, unwashed and unkempt. My body was sunburned and my lips blistered and swollen. Other than the blinding, roasting midday sunlight, the most powerful sensation by far was the slow, fractious creaking sound of wood against wood as the ship experienced the power and force of the jostling sea.

XV

Not everything can be explained. There is thought and so there is reason, and so there is hope. But as thought itself is non-atomic and therefore devoid of any concrete manifested practical virtue, strictly speaking its ability to affect society is through behavior.

As I descended the stairwell from the roof door down to my apartment I was startled to discover Detective Mullen leaning in the shadows outside my door, sporting an olive wool trench coat and smoking a filterless cigarette as always. He waited until I was directly in front of him to suddenly spin me around, pushing me roughly against the door and grabbing my wrists to handcuff me from behind. He quickly muttered, "Richard Steele, you're under arrest for sexual assault," then went on to read me my rights. In just moments I found myself in the back of his unmarked sedan. He informed me that one Penelope Furr had pressed charges against me. I was questioned in a dark, musty interrogation room for the next two hours, and then thrown in a cell for the night. Upon being afforded the opportunity to make one telephone call I immediately rang a colleague of mine, Marvin Thalenberg.

As it transpired, I didn't even need him as they had no factual evidence of any kind other than an accusation by Furr and a line-up in which I was compelled to participate. I held up a number 2 but she pegged some poor bastard with the number 6 whom they led away as he protested fruitlessly.

This past Tuesday my psychologist shared with me "The Five Habits of Mind" by Deborah Meier. I'm not sure what the exact purpose of it was in and of itself; I suspected it was directed towards minimizing one's sense of paranoia via logical applications, which would be absurd *if* those impulses are at least even marginally psychotic in nature. She had obviously applied it as a self-serving analytical tool in an initial attempt to determine the basis of my claim of having seen the body in question in the park.

Habit one, evidence: How do we know what is true and false? What evidence counts? How sure can we be? What makes it credible to us? (This includes using the scientific method and more.)

To my mind I had told her it is for one obviously a good way to dispel or at least reduce paranoia, fear, jealously, envy. I myself have issues with the scientific method however as it suggests in effect that unless one can prove someone's idea it cannot be accepted as "true." This becomes complicated quickly in part because the idea of "true" versus "fact" begs for its distinction to be clarified, vis-à-vis a fact is essentially a "condition," event or action in the present or past that can be or was memorialized, predicated often on the idea of multiple witnesses; a truth on the other hand is typically either based on observation and recordation, or in many cases is merely a subjective assessment not necessarily measurable or qualified via information. Therefore the questions within this "evidence" habit are almost rhetorical with regards to how they make their point: just because there's no evidence does not necessarily mean something is not true (happening); it may simply be that one has not happened to either discover or stumble upon that evidence yet. (Simply put, we know that things are happening that we do not know about specifically; therefore, it is a truth that facts exist that we do not have knowledge of—one does not require the use of the scientific method to prove it.)

Habit two, viewpoint: How else might this look like if we stepped into other shoes? If we were looking at it from a different direction? If we had a different history or expectation?

This requires the exercise of informed "empathy" and imagination. It requires flexibility of mind. This is a logical extension and sequence of "evidence."

Habit three, connections/cause and effect: Is there a pattern? Have we seen something like this before? What are the possible consequences?

This is coercive by the therapist in that of course our initial answer to these questions is yes, and yes ... most paranoia and other forms of fear would seem to me to be either repetitive/recurring or essentially constant. I suppose the idea here is that if we recognize a pattern in our own behavior it might be something that others may notice willy-nilly and if so, being quite possibly embarrassing we may wish to suppress this behavior in favor of more "acceptable" social behavior—but, that is treating the symptom and not the cause, so the value in recognizing any negative behavioral patterns short of effective corrective therapy will be limited.

Habit four, conjecture: Could it have been otherwise? Supposing that? What if ... ? This habit requires use of the imagination as well as knowledge of alternative possibilities. It includes the habits described above.

Everything could have been otherwise (events can only be manifested in reality by two things; their perception by individuals cognitively and by "non-events"); that is, events can only exist as long as the potential for "no event" within either that time frame and/or particular perceptive manifestation exists, i.e., nothing is happening arguably constitutes the absence of an event. (Since the idea that nothing may actually exist cannot be proven by the scientific method, conversely we have no way of proving anything does exist with the method.) So to my mind, this habit suggests a value in simply rethinking either what someone did, or how they approached a situation, or both. While it's painfully obvious the exercise may be helpful.

Habit five, relevance: Does it matter? Who cares?

That's the whole problem: once we decide that something matters/mattered, it matters, i.e. we have placed prima facie value on it. So, if it has negative implications either by sheer virtue of its nature or by how we reacted to it or addressed it, the idea of "what mattered" is then transformed into the idea of a "problem." As for "who cares," this is a good "grounding tool" for the sake of more realistic perspective on a matter than we may be placing on it at a given time.

In conclusion I told her it seems to me that these are simple fundamental behavioral characteristics of an essentially grounded person. The real question then may actually be: is there any value in them to acting them out, or are they only truly transforming if we evolve them into instinctive habits or behaviors? If it's the latter then I have much work to do.

XVI

III. VERE FORSIT

Wittgenstein purposefully ignored the fundamental ideal of reality. His focus in Tractatus was mainly on the inter-dynamics of language as it relates to philosophy and as such, the work lacks context other than essential legitimate theory.

It strikes me there are three realities as relates to the cognitive human mind. At the core and unadulterated by thought there is the horrific "ignored reality" which encompasses virtually everything that we do not wish to consciously consider: things scatological; death, waste, carnage, mutilation, genocide and the like. They are a constant and permanent part of our daily lives yet we compartmentalize them in order to be able to bear living. There is also a "collective perception" encompassing all things bearable to pleasant—this is the general state of mind in which we choose to live our lives. The third reality, "fantasy," is the world in which we imagine what our lives would be if we could have things our way. Experienced in periodic bursts—whether acted out or imagined—it is blended into our otherwise mundane overall existence so as to enhance the general quality of our daily lives. Embraced consistently however, the person is neurotic, psychotic or insane depending on the intensity and scope of the fantasies at hand. Ironically however the latter often includes the undeniable perversities of the "ignored reality" which the rest of us lack the courage to live through. This is the foundation of the collective cowardice that is essential to the coping ability of all humanity.

XVII

I parked my nondescript compact car along the gravel shoulder two houses down from the boss's house. It was a more upscale neighborhood than Mullen's of course but it had that same listless, weighted down feeling common to virtually all suburbs reflecting the numbed, unspoken emotional agreement between its residents to produce and consume. Outside the front door I encountered that ubiquitous random collection of footwear that accompanies bourgeois house parties. Everyone inside, particularly the females had taken some time earlier that day to select shoes in which they would be socially accepted while achieving at least a reasonable level of comfort. Instead of playing some generally acceptable if commercial music like Michael Buble, Abba or even something as innocuous as Bocelli, my boss had a CD running as I entered the house of Bruckner's fourth symphony. I'm sure he didn't even know what it was, his wife probably had put it on in a calculated attempt to evoke an "intelligent" environment for the evening. The brass continued to bother me; if the second and third trumpets were playing on the staff the horns would sound muddy, not enough range between the parts as harmonized. This added to my tension and so after briefly thanking them insincerely for the invitation I quickly moved towards the makeshift bar in the living room.

Various people from our office were there, for one. I immediately spotted our obese receptionist whom people admired for her "joviality," which I thought was nothing more than a constant, desperate attempt to mask her general unfortunate predicament. There was a tall middle-aged Asian woman for whom my hostess held the greatest admiration: she was the daughter of a retired businessman who owned commercial buildings downtown in which several major broadcasting stations were located. I couldn't understand why I should admire her for this for any reason whatsoever. When one of my colleagues from the firm approached me with his wife and launched into a seemingly endless description of their plans to re-landscape the grounds of their home I found myself drifting instantly into an altered state of consciousness within which my senses, devoid of any actual stimulus relative to the ideas and objects which my mind spontaneously conjured, nevertheless instantly spawned virgin impressions which, penetrating my sensory integuments with effortless abandon provided irrefutable alternative stimulation under the circumstances. At one point, under the sudden, terrific weight of an agoraphobic attack while in the center of the crowded living room I excused myself from a couple of nobodies and made for the kitchen which I had spotted over the heads of many due to the constant entries and exits of the catering staff. Just as I approached the slightly less trafficked periphery of the area a waiter approached me with a tray of cold hors d'oeuvres which disgusted me at first sight: some sort of minced seafood concoction impossible to identify or categorize pretentiously presented on the tray in individual spoons with arched handles. Upon my arrival earlier my host had proudly explained to me that the culinary theme for the evening was French; he informed me that he belonged to a group of attorneys in the city who shared an interest in European wines and that this evening's selections were paired to the food at-hand. No sooner had he mentioned all this than two of his wine club colleagues appeared on either side of us nodding their heads in support of his comments, obviously having been snooping nearby and looking for a point affording them entry to the conversation. They were bores; I did not recognize them as prior acquaintances within the local legal industry. As my boss had said that he had asked the chef to apply a "modern touch" to the menu as opposed to "Escoffier," the shorter one made a minor crack about avoiding fluted mushrooms and cream sauces. I asked in a teasing manner if they were familiar with the general prevailing cultural and social norms of the *Belle Epoche* as they would relate contextually to the cuisine of Paris particularly during the time of that great chef; they silently glanced at each other and moved away, parting company with me along with my irritated boss.

I wasn't there very long at all before my cell phone rang. It was an administrative woman at the police precinct, a Ms.

Williams calling on behalf of Detective Mullen. She told me that there was a new development in the case of the body in the park and that it was "good news." She told me that I should come over to the stationhouse right away so that they could share the information with me. I told her that I was at a party and so would come by within the next couple of hours. I wondered what it could be.

XVIII

At night I am sometimes visited by a lovely middle-aged Chinese woman named Moon who stands at my bedside in a simple, shimmery blood red dress. She is calm, reserved, with all the tranquility and timeless calm of Quin Yan. Moon is elegant and poised. She reminds me of my mother, my mother devoid of any maternal relationship with me. Last night I awoke around two a.m. to find her gazing down at me serenely, a delicate, loving smiling barely traceable on her lips. She told me that I should beware a flock of blackbirds. That was all. There was an ominous overtone to her admonition but I sensed it as a kind of destiny, which was not only unavoidable but also in fact good.

She last appeared before me three nights ago. I awakened slowly, sensing something, and gazed up with squinting eyes to see her usual warm, comforting smile as she looked down at me with loving energy. She was very beautiful, but at any moment when my mind would slip to imagining her nakedness, her carnal intricacies, she would instantly disappear via strobe-like flashes like an image in an antique flip-book where random pages had been torn out. She sang me what sounded like an ancient Chinese folk song, gently, mellifluously and with profound calm. This was the energy and inspiration I needed to face the coming day.

XIX

Mullen sat on a cheap folding aluminum chair in the depressing little interrogation room, smoking a cigarette. I turned my head, nodding upwards towards a small "No Smoking" sign on the wall to his right; he reached up with his right hand and tore it down, tossing it into a metal trash receptacle under the little Formica table that separated us. He informed me that in their ongoing investigation into my original claim, a security surveillance video had been recovered from a parking garage directly across the street from the park where I had been sitting when I allegedly saw the corpse.

He turned towards a small old television atop a side table in the corner of the stark white room and reaching up with remote in hand pushed a button to play a recording of what they had discovered. As the tape began playing, Benz stepped silently into the room to join us, standing just behind me while leaning into the opposite corner. I immediately recognized myself seated on the park bench; after a moment I turned to my left, gazing towards a cluster of shrubs about twenty feet away. Passersby occasionally passed across the front of the screen in either direction, preoccupied with wherever they might have been going. My head remained turned for a good minute or so before looking down, pausing and then standing up as my stare then returned to the direction of the bushes. I then appeared to walk absentmindedly away, yet never taking my eyes off the area in question. Mullen hit the playback button, running the footage back rapidly and then just as quickly hitting the play button until pausing the image midway and zooming in on the area of the shrubs. There was nothing there but the grass around them.

I was told I was being charged with fraud. There would also be expenses involved related to the necessary investigation regarding my claim involving payroll and administrative activities. I would eventually be arraigned but in the meanwhile would be free on my own recognizance, the only stipulation being the immediate surrender of my passport for obvious reasons.

XX

The following night I tried to unwind a bit and so headed over to the Princeton Club after work, ensconcing myself in the dusty old library amongst leather bound tomes and disheveled newspapers. The very first headline raised my eyebrows: "Fledgling Actress Possibly Pushed Down Stairs to Her Death ..."

Wittgenstein was undoubtedly a fundamentally insecure person: while he aggressively preached and tested his new philosophy out on a captive and impressionable student audience at Oxford he simultaneously pleaded with them not to bother studying the classical western philosophical canon of Sophocles all the way through Locke, Hume, Spinoza, the Danes and the budding existentialists of the period. While he was long-obsessed with the idea of the inherent materialism of language tragically and ironically suppressing selective expressive thought, to a good extent later in life he second-guessed himself at the risk of suggesting that virtually all his earlier work was flawed—it having been largely based on the idea that language was sufficiently formidable in its range and intellectual fluency not only to communicate philosophy but to govern it.

If one is to accept his idea of subject/predicate declaration as proof of fact, i.e., the dog is big, the sky is blue, the man was mean, the body was on the grass etc. then one is also able to imagine a picture of the event expressed. To imagine is to create, and whether one imagines that picture as the one who declared it or from the perspective of the observer, each participant creates an image in his own mind of the *same idea*—whether or not he agrees with it as a truth. But Wittgenstein declared in effect that the picture *is* a truth because it exists, or that is to say, the picture bears certain truthfulness in and of itself based simply on the fact that it exists at all. This is not to suggest a "noble" truth; only a truth in that it is truthful that the *thought* now exists; it is *something*. What I saw that day in the park is a truth: not only because I saw it but also because the moment I declared it to the detectives they pictured it and so it existed for them as well. Therefore they were not actually looking to confirm an *alleged* truth; they were seeking to validate my assertion, as they do not think in the way of Wittgenstein. If a scientist sees a fish on a table he knows it is a fish. If he then chooses to examine a piece of that fish under the microscope he will observe minute details of the fish but he already knows it is a fish. Wittgenstein would not have needed to insist upon habeas corpus, he would have understood the picture I saw at face value: as a picture it was real and so I saw it and he would realize that.

The detectives therefore had needed to confirm an actual body in order to equate my claim to their level of "truth" *a priori.* Over time laws have been written with sufficient specificity to disallow within society a declaration related to a crime that cannot be substantiated. According to them I am guilty of such a crime as a *substitute* for a fundamental crime. The laws of any modern society relating to violent crime are conceived and enforced based on fear: fear that such a crime can actually happen to the individual embodying that fear—that is who writes the law to address it.

In his heart, every man has slain his mother a thousand times. I am no exception—although to do so is certainly not a crime. But I have not ever, and will never be charged with this crime because it is only an *idea*. Whether or not is a "good" idea is irrelevant. Such ideas in the very least are "valid" ideas as they represent unadulterated reactions to human conditions—such reactions we are permitted within the sphere of fallible human thought. The extent to which one weighs them out with respect to the morals and principles of common society will determine one's ability—and permissibility—to be allowed to continue to function within that society with conventional freedoms. As such my freedoms have now been threatened.

According to the article, Penelope Furr was murdered the same evening I saw her leaving the Irish pub with those people unknown to me. Theoretically I should immediately report what I saw that night to the proper authorities, yet given my experience with them to-date I would not even consider the thought; they would think me mad.

XXI

Regardless of these various circumstances I remained determined to continue on with my deconstruction of *Tractatus*. As eventually Wittgenstein confessed to the work having been flawed, one might regard my efforts as merely working out the details of his self-conjecture *post facto*. At any rate, everyone eventually becomes a victim of the world's injustice and I am no exception. I must use time to my advantage and to complete my work while it is still possible.

Wittgenstein went on to elaborate on his "picture theory," a group of beliefs central to his overall belief in the extreme gravitas of language as a philosophical platform:

> *If a fact is to be a picture, it must have something in common with what it depicts. There must be something identical in a picture and what it depicts, to enable the one to be a picture of the other at all. What a picture must have in common with reality, in order to be able to depict it—correctly or incorrectly—in the way that it does, is its pictorial form. A picture can depict any reality whose form it has. A spatial picture can depict anything spatial, a coloured one anything coloured, etc. A picture cannot,*

however, depict its pictorial form: it displays it. A picture represents its subject from a position outside it. (Its standpoint is its representational form.) That is why a picture represents its subject correctly or incorrectly. A picture cannot, however, place itself outside its representational form. What any picture, of whatever form, must have in common with reality, in order to be able to depict it—correctly or incorrectly—in any way at all, is logical form, i.e. the form of reality. A picture whose pictorial form is logical form is called a logical picture. Every picture is at the same time a logical one. (On the other hand, not every picture is, for example, a spatial one.) Logical pictures can depict the world. A picture has logico-pictorial form in common with what it depicts. A picture depicts reality by representing a possibility of existence and non-existence of states of affairs. A picture contains the possibility of the situation that it represents. A picture agrees with reality or fails to agree; it is correct or incorrect, true or false.

What a picture represents it represents independently of its truth or falsity, by means of its pictorial form. What a picture represents is its sense. The agreement or dis-agreement or its sense with reality constitutes its truth or falsity. In order to tell whether a picture is true or false we must compare it with reality. It is impossible to tell from the picture alone whether it is true or false. There are no pictures that are true a priori. A logical picture of facts is a thought. "A state of affairs is thinkable": what this means is that we can picture it to ourselves. The totality of true thoughts is a picture of the world.

A thought contains the possibility of the situation of which it is the thought. What is thinkable is possible too. Thought can never be of anything illogical, since, if it were, we should have to think illogically. It used to be said that God could create anything except what would be contrary to the laws of logic. The truth is that we could not say what an "illogical" world would look like.

There is a certain *rhythm* to language, one that ironically plays itself out most conspicuously to those who do not know the language at all. This is the audio undulation as it were that provides each language its organic foundation of communication upon which specific ideas may be laid out in intellectual counterpoint to the musical pulse beneath it. Wittgenstein failed to recognize this aspect of language, or at least to consider its role as a marker in relation to his deconstruction of linguistic elements relative to the expression of philosophical ideas. It is as important as words and ideas themselves in that the shifting tonalities formed by strings of words collectively espousing ideas would not have the same meaning in the absence of such inflections.

XXII

"Logical form ... 'the form of reality.' " So said Wittgenstein. The expression both intrigues and repulses me. Is it even conceivable that such a profound thought leader could suggest that logic is "acceptable" in and of itself as long as it conforms to a present reality—whether or not that particular reality *itself* is logical?! If so then for one, my visits to Mullen's house were perfectly logical in that they constituted a behavioral expression of the reality that I invoked. Here I agree with Wittgenstein—or at least, it suits my purpose.

I ordered another bourbon from the irreverent club waiter and put pen to paper to develop my response to Wittgenstein's sacrosanct picture theory, only to stop almost immediately: the theory makes perfect sense to me after all—it is a legitimate and logical depicter of my own reality. Given that, I shall now proceed to picture my future.

XXIII

It was before seven o'clock the following morning when the pounding on my apartment door began. About that time in the early winter there is a narrow band of rich golden light that strikes the old plaster wall as sunlight penetrates my bedroom chamber between the rose-colored drapes over my bed. This panoply of light and sound met me with painful contradiction as I awoke to a confusion of senses and imminent threat. It took only several whirling, frenzied minutes for me to be arrested, dressed, handcuffed and led out to their waiting squad car, charged in the death of Penelope Furr.

Thalenberg arrived at the stationhouse within just thirty minutes following my call demanding to know from Mullen or Benz the basis upon which they had executed my arrest. They were a good thirty feet down the cinderblock corridor from my holding cell speaking in animated voices but too far away for me to make them out clearly. What I did discern was that he was demanding to know what specific evidence they had tying me to the crime. In the article it had said that the bartender at a popular theatre district pub last saw Furr. I realized then that if I still were to report my story from that night it would corroborate with that of the pub employee, but being that it was already public information I would likely be accused of making it all up. Shortly thereafter Thalenberg returned to debrief me and upon hearing my recounting of that evening he advised me against saying anything: he pointed out that my prior impromptu tryst with the victim would cause a whole new level of investigation of me and my potential involvement.

I asked him to get me some bourbon but that of course was not permitted. He had left me the early edition of the local paper and in it there was a rather lengthy article on the background of Penelope Furr. I could say it was interesting but then quite often "interesting" would be better referred to simply as "unfamiliar." Ingesting information—whether interesting or not—is naturally laborious in that the mind must work to process the new information, it must masticate ideas. The story was predictable but then so was she. She came to this eastern metropolis from a small house and a small family with a small-minded, if at least rather unoriginal dream: to become a recognized actress. Bourgeois background, father a union worker in some bleak industrial facility; her mother a mother. So here she was in the big city and after a random night of performance, drinks and some reasonable amount of revelry she was shoved down a staircase in her walk-up pre-war apartment building after arguing with a stranger over the idea of having a nightcap or not. There were no witnesses to the crime.

XXIV

I deduced that given no direct witnesses my chance of being released was quite plausible. I thought back on that rainy night when I first encountered Penelope Furr. She was certainly not lost in Milton's "limbo of vanity"—although she nevertheless lacked even the most fundamental carriage of grace at the core. But what of Milton now?! It was I who now stood at the breach of his wall of heaven.

While Thalenberg had not yet returned to inform me of what possible evidence they might be prepared to claim against me, I consoled myself in the thought that likely any DNA from our one carnal encounter was now far to old to be recovered. As such, I am here based on suspicion, and only that. Gazing up at the plain white ceiling of my cell at 2 AM one night I recalled words of Wittgenstein that shed light on my ability to achieve calm in the midst of my current dramatic predicament: "The child learns by believing the adult. Doubt comes after belief." It therefore seems inevitable that, in providing information to children and given that a great amount of information is incorrect (for various reasons) in and of itself, it is inevitable that adults eventually corrupt their own children. Am I therefore at risk of losing my freedom or worse merely by virtue of the fact that I am fundamentally misinformed?

When I was a child my mother repeatedly advised me that regardless of almost any conceivable calamity I possessed a unique capability for survival. It is with this exceptional confidence in mind that I am not in the least bit thwarted or even fearful in my present circumstances. Freedom is the supreme portal to pleasure and pleasure is the nucleus of hope in every human being. By denying freedom one denies his victim pleasure. That, not confinement, is the true weapon of incarceration. The productive impact of punishment is inherently governed by the amount of freedom at stake following one's successful completion of the punishment prescribed. If I am to have no hope of a pleasurable existence thereafter then I am not intimidated by my conditions of today.

In my youth, the fact that my mother was a mute had profound impact on our family dynamic—she had to establish and sustain her matriarchal role through the power of silence. In the end her commitment and passion trumped and transcended the million lost words of my father. When I think of her now, I envisage her as if sitting for a portrait, always silent, always calm.

I may no longer be a child but I am a person whose core beliefs as well as many ancillary, random ones were inculcated in me by adults—my parents, teachers and others, even in some cases by my early enemies. With age and experience comes wisdom in its many infinite and immeasurable forms. And if doubt is the mother of wisdom—skepticism, circumspection, innate suspicion—I am now a very wise man. Can the same be said of those who by virtue of ignorance and fear have worked to entrap me? Wittgenstein remarked: "I learned an enormous amount and then accepted it on human authority, and then I found some things confirmed or disconfirmed by my own experience." Such is my fate as of this hour.

XXV

I strode in a leisurely gait down the pristine strand of powdered sand that tapered away magnificently before me into a serpentine wisp. The waters of the tropical gulf were calm, rippling gently under the touch of a supple summer breeze. Moon had come to me the night before in my cell and taken my hand to lead me to this beach. Her blood-red silk crimson gown contrasted severely against the blurred aquamarine waters and blinding white shoreline before us. She talked to me, calmed me. Moon suggested that I had nothing to fear no matter how things turned out with my arrest or indictment. We stopped and stood together, our bare feet caressed by the cool foamy ocean waters. I stood shorter than her and gently laid my cheek against her soft, warm breast and closed my eyes. I could feel her heart beating slowly and rhythmically. Her skin smelled of bergamot, saffron, sweet lavender. Light faint raindrops were falling upon us. For the first time I knew that bliss was not a mood but simply rather one particular state of inspired consciousness.

XXVI

My cell window set into the center of its western wall is a simple deep opening between the weighty cinderblocks that comprise it. It is only the size of a small book, but gazing into it I have a view to the entire world. Through it I can see the sun and the moon, feel the temperature of the air and even smell fresh bread being baked in the adjacent staff kitchen. These sensory experiences provide fuel for my imagination and liberate my spirit from the stark confines of my cubicle and those who keep me here.

Today Thalenberg stopped by and left me a copy of the daily paper that had another article on Penelope Furr's background, this time a human-interest story praising her love for the stage and revealing her extinguished dreams of eventual stardom. Artists' reputations tend to improve after death, but particularly following suicide. She should have considered that option earlier on. He also brought me an unmarked manila folder that he opened melodramatically upon a small metal table that the guard placed for him in the center of my cell. In it were various black and white photographs of her body at the foot of the stairs. The last image—one which he tossed atop the pile, was taken from above her as she lay on her stomach in a black trench coat, left arm broken backwards and beneath her, face to one side staring blankly back at life while a trickle of dark blood sprang from her open mouth. I suspected he was testing me for my reaction but I remained expressionless as I felt nothing.

As time progressed, sitting in my cell I began to experience unparalleled freedom. Gazing up at the rectangular borders of the old plaster ceiling I recognized the infinite length of the lines that defined it. They reached far beyond the confines of this city and the farthest reaches of my dreams. They resonated with the fears and passions of the occupants they were inadvertently assigned to contain and cast outwardly the defective qualities of the system that imposed them.

XXVII

Several weeks ago new evidence was presented by the prosecutor's office which they claimed further implicated me in the murder of Penelope Furr. At night I sit on my bed in the darkness listening softly to Mahler's eighth symphony. I find particular solace in the closing adagio choral movement; it transports me to higher places which by virtue of their intrinsic beauty exclude people. On some evenings Moon joins me in my cell and we listen together for hours on end. That is when I am now most content.

XXVIII

It has now been almost seven weeks since I was first jailed.
A man who has violated the laws of society has effectively
failed society but not necessarily himself. Morals are of the
masses, ethics the provenance of the individual. With this in
mind I am further convinced of the legitimacy of my current
disposition and the absurdity of my current situation notwithstanding the subjective judgment of others. Wittgenstein
addressed this effectively in terms of ethical conundrums.

> *When an ethical law of the form, "Thou shalt ..." is laid down,
> one's first thought is, "And what if I do not do it?" It is clear,
> however, that ethics has nothing to do with punishment and
> reward in the usual sense of the terms. So our question about
> the consequences of an action must be unimportant.—At least
> those consequences should not be events. For there must be
> something right about the question we posed. There must
> indeed be some kind of ethical reward and ethical
> punishment, but they must reside in the action itself. (And it is
> also clear that the reward must be something pleasant and the
> punishment something unpleasant.)*

Eventually Thalenberg was able to gain permission to supply me with certain objects and materials that I requested for the purpose of sustaining mental stimulation under these exceptional and protracted circumstances. In addition to several writing tablets, pencils and erasers, a small desk of sorts was placed in the far eastern corner of my cell along with a Spartan yet acceptable office chair. Finally and most importantly, he was able to locate and bring to me from my apartment my four Wittgenstein texts. A modest metal desk lamp was also provided, although that, along with the pencils was removed each evening before lights out in order to discourage self-harm.

I will no longer simply transcribe for you the *Tractatus* in full sections—rather, I will take the liberty of adding my own comments into the pages themselves where I feel it important to make a point or wage an argument or objection; my fate is unclear and as time is in turn as well, I will struggle to complete my contributions to what Proust deemed the "permanent and the significant" with a sense of general urgency.

An expression presupposes the forms of all the propositions in which it can occur. It is the common characteristic mark of a class of propositions. It is therefore presented by means of the general form of the propositions that it characterizes. In fact, in this form the expression will be constant and everything else variable. Thus an expression is presented by means of a variable whose values are the propositions that contain the expression. (In the limiting case the variable becomes a constant, the expression becomes a proposition.) I call such a variable a "propositional variable." An expression has meaning only in a proposition. All variables can be construed as propositional variables. (Even variable names.)

This is not entirely correct. If I were to say "I am tired" it by nature may be judged a preposition yet it is also a condition and therefore a fact. But if an element of doubt is by nature part of the expression as in "I think I'm tired," then it may or may not be a fact even though it has been expressed (therefore an "expression") and may also be a condition. Accordingly, not every fact represents an expression. For example, "that's hot" is not only possibly an expression; it is also possibly a fact and also an observation. But if it is a fact then it is no longer merely a proposition in and of itself. This also reveals that none of the three respective qualities or characteristics of an expression—an expression, a fact or an observation—are mutually exclusive whatsoever. Mathematics would substantiate that there are many diverse combinations of these three qualities—but more importantly that their combinations do not necessarily always directly correlate with the particular nature and verifiability of a given expression. Wittgenstein seems to excuse these variable possibilities in the following paragraph but treats them in a manner conducive to his core theory.

*If we turn a constituent of a proposition into a variable,
there is a class of propositions all of which are values of the
resulting variable proposition. In general, this class too will
be dependent on the meaning that our arbitrary
conventions have given to parts of the original proposition.
But if all the signs in it that have arbitrarily determined
meanings are turned into variables, we shall still get a class
of this kind. This one, however, is not dependent on any
convention, but solely on the nature of the pro position. It
corresponds to a logical form—a logical prototype. What
values a propositional variable may take is something that is
stipulated. The stipulation of values is the variable. To
stipulate values for a propositional variable is to give the
propositions whose common characteristic the variable is.
The stipulation is a description of those propositions. The
stipulation will therefore be concerned only with symbols,
not with their meaning. And the only thing essential to the
stipulation is that it is merely a description of symbols and
states nothing about what is signified. How the description
of the propositions is produced is not essential.*

By happenstance this is a brilliant confirmation and
extension of the Chinese Room Paradox: if one cannot
understand, speak or read Chinese whatsoever but is taught
to associate a certain specific thought with each of a group
of Chinese written characters, it is conceivable that he can
nevertheless function and survive at least to a fundamental
degree purely by utilizing the association between his needs

and the given "symbols" (abstract to him) in order to obtain various things. If he wants water for example, presenting a Chinese character which actually means "rock" but taught to him to as representing water in hand he can simply point to it to request water. What the original paradox does not contain as a part of its explanatory proposition/discussion however is the possibility that the subject may not know—or at least be sure, if each of the given associations taught to him are correct in their correlations.

Like Frege and Russell I construe a proposition as a function of the expressions contained in it. A sign is what can be perceived of a symbol. So one and the same sign (written or spoken, etc.) can be common to two different symbols—in which case they will signify in different ways. Our use of the same sign to signify two different objects can never indicate a common characteristic of the two, if we use it with two different modes of signification. For the sign, of course, is arbitrary. So we could choose two different signs instead, and then what would be left in common on the signifying side? In everyday language it very frequently happens that the same word has different modes of signification—and so belongs to different symbols—or that two words that have different modes of signification are employed in propositions in what is superficially the same way. Thus the word "is" figures as the copula, as a sign for identity, and as an expression for existence; "exist" figures as an intransitive verb like "go," and "identical" as an adjective; we speak of something, but also of something's happening. (In the proposition, "Green is green"—where the first word is the proper name of a person and the last an adjective—these words do not merely have different meanings: they are different symbols.) In this way the most fundamental confusions are easily produced (the whole of philosophy is full of them). In order to avoid such errors we must make use of a sign-language that excludes them by not using the same sign for different symbols and by not using in a superficially similar way signs that have different modes of signification: that is to say, a sign-language that is governed by logical grammar—by logical syntax. (The conceptual notation of Frege and Russell is such a language, though, it is true, it fails to exclude all mistakes.)

Ultimately, whether a "language" is expressed by visual symbols or via the spoken word, each symbol or utterance has in common that it is a "symbol" that represents an idea, or the notion of an idea i.e., an object, etc. Accordingly, if Wittgenstein's "sign language" had a different symbol for his two different meanings (representations) for the word "green," it is likely that the end-thought intended is very much the same and as such will be perceived by the recipient as having essentially the same meaning. As such, this idea of Wittgenstein that his solution might come closer to addressing the core problem of philosophy ironically reinforces it due to his projecting philosophical "solutions" of a purely theoretical/intellectual argumentative approach that hold no practical value even for one who might believe in it. Unless philosophical ideas in and of themselves possess sufficient practicality to offer actionable constructive solutions within society, they hold no true value beyond theoretical folly.

XXIX

As a child I was stricken with a severe and debilitating attack of meningitis and hospitalized throughout my second year. My single remaining recollection is of walking down a long, empty and sterile white corridor while holding the pinky of a female duty nurse. We would enter what seemed a vast lavatory, all its surfaces finished in white, blazing fluorescent lights above and ultraviolet strip lights lining each toilet seat, casting ghostly lavender bands across the inside walls of the vacant stalls. I fear that something dark and damaging may have touched my life there, a psychological infection trumping the love and salvation I had otherwise simultaneously experienced.

It is difficult to successfully mine the roots of ones own adult agony as relates to past experiences that may constitute a shrouded yet undeniable platform for current behavioral toxicity. I store my memories in clear glass jars. My periodic amnesia is much like a wall that blocks my ability to return to the past with a view towards coercing the future. Only occasionally does my memory return to provide me a door to what was and what may have long ago made me what I am in moments unbeknownst to me.

XXX

I have a vision of Penelope Furr on the last night of her life in this world. Her small, modest flat is a rear second-floor unit accessible only via a wooden staircase reached through a short alleyway from the adjacent tree-lined boulevard. She was clearly inebriated by the time she returned home but nevertheless ascended the stairs to her doorway competently. Startled as she initially was to turn and encounter her unexpected visitor, they did after a brief exchange proceed together into her residence.

What would Wittgenstein say here under these circumstances? I picture him sitting here on a lone metal stool in the center of the empty cell looking like *The Thinker* by Rodin. If one could hear the symphony of language and comprehend its bottomless depths of nuance and majesty one could begin to penetrate the soul of Wittgenstein. Wittgenstein asserted that ethics has nothing to do with punishment and reward in the usual sense, but rather, thought there must be some kind of ethical reward and punishment lying in the action itself. Such a thought gave me great ongoing comfort, knowing that the full circle of experience relating to her death was already complete and whole.

XXXI

My daily breakfast is normally dropped off to my cell by the elderly Albanian guard named Sammy Eisuf, but this morning the dismal tray was pushed through the narrow slot in the bars by a lean redheaded man with a disengaged, forlorn expression. Our eyes met only ever so briefly but in his gaze I felt the collective weight of the energy of punishment.

I asked Thalenberg to bring for me from my home my small-framed print of St. John the Evangelist by Piero di Cosimo. I find great solace in this work. St. John is youthfully portrayed, seemingly androgynous and not intimidated by the chalice before him where a poisonous snake lurks just below. Purportedly, St. John once sipped wine laced with poison in a faith demonstration following the deaths of others whose spiritual convictions failed to trump the effects of such a lethal solution. I find it enchanting: for me, enchantment is a collective human emotion shepherded forth between willing souls who share a rapturous vulnerability to beauty. I am reminded by this piece that we do not actually "discover" art—rather, it is cast forth independently of any specific audience and not for audience's sake but for reasons that vary widely and will only ever be completely known to the artist himself, if at all. The viewer or collector performs an act after-the-fact; his interaction with the art—whether via acquisition or merely by contemplation does not change the creation itself; it is a personal love affair mysterious as such which will always remain the private purview of the creator. A person can never truly understand the very nature of his own creation—it is the result, or victim as it were, of circumstances. As a portrayal of circumstance the art and the viewer have these things in common. In these ways I experience a symbiotic, oedipal chemistry with this portrait of the saint. I have only these two friends now, and they exemplify the fact that friendship is really only an *idea* conjured up randomly as the result of arbitrary, unanticipated feelings.

XXXII

I am incarcerated by virtue of the law and I am an expert at the law, yet none of my legal knowledge can help me now in any way—unless I am to represent myself. But I will let Thalenberg take care of all of that. I am no longer interested in my defense or in regaining my physical freedom. In retrospect, my initial, almost frantic desire for liberation was more based on Maslovian survival tenets than any actual desire. If the great philosophers expected that they should be able to save us, then should we expect to be saved? They have failed *Aut via:* nothing they have said or done has proved effective enough to save me from my current predicament, either by influence upon me or my captors.

There is a black man in the cell to my right. He is going to be executed some time soon. He simply sits, all day, every day on the same spot on the edge of his cot staring off into space. He is mainly upset because upon his arrival six weeks ago he learned that smoking is prohibited in the facility for health reasons. As a capital punishment inmate he finds this objectionable. Ironically, our guards all have to step outside to smoke on their breaks. On my other side the cell has remained empty, otherwise looking identical to my own. When I look at it from within the bars of mine it is like a photograph depicting the quality and confines of my own existence.

Thalenberg came by today and left me a small package wrapped in plain brown paper. I opened it early evening and discovered it to be a slim paperback: *Four Quartets* by T.S. Eliot. I also had Thalenberg retrieve from my residence an acetate recording of Ravel's *Concerto for the Left Hand*, written for Wittgenstein's brother who lost his right arm in the Second World War. With a new handicap one's behavior is altered by the fusion of his mind's coping and practical inclinations as mitigated by the vastly diminished limits of his physical capabilities. The intermittent pop and hiss of the old record spinning at a rate visually in excess of the pace of the somber music itself created a meditative energy for me as I gazed at it serenely for long periods to pass the time. Wittgenstein's assertion regarding the natural limitations of value allowed me to better understand my current plight and the fact that, regardless of my actual role in any key events impacting my life or others', I was naturally exonerated not only from guilt but *responsibility* by sheer virtue of the anterior essence of "values":

> *The sense of the world must lie outside the world. In the world everything is as it is, and everything happens as it does happen: in it no value exists—and if it did exist, it would have no value. If there is any value that does have value, it must lie outside the whole sphere of what happens and is the case. For all that happens and is the*

case is accidental. What makes it non-accidental cannot lie within the world, since if it did it would itself be accidental. It must lie outside the world.

My fear is frankly greater when on my rooftop, teetering many floors up above the street than here at risk of death by another's hand; it is the mettle of the actual decision that bears more gravitas on the subject than the act itself. Ultimately, death by one's own hand is far more complete than that by any other.

XXXIII

Today I contemplated nothing but olfactory sensations, past and present. I recalled the rich, antique aspects of Mrs. Mullen's *sauce bourguignon*, if that was indeed what it was—and that conjoined, obscure sentimental quality provoked by the smell of sautéed shallots or garlic detected at first subliminally from some distant room in an old family home late on some winter afternoon past at that hour when chartreuse sunlight rapidly wanes and the cooling air coaxes the inhabitants indoors to commingle and eventually retire together, enveloped and cosseted within the darkness that ensues. Sitting in my small library room on late fall evenings, I used to enjoy the spanky-rude nose of fine charred barrel bourbon, contemplating the obvious yet indefinable harmony of the liquid's radiant amber hue and the enchanted smoky scent it evoked.

There is however a disturbing, almost alarming quality to the artificial citrus scent of the murky cleaning liquid splashed randomly about by the mop of the prison janitor as he makes his morning rounds here at daybreak. This in cacophonous contrast to the alluring currents of yeast off the crust of fresh breakfast loafs being finished off in the ovens some floors below me within the building.

XXXIV

Moon and I walk together for miles at a time down the serene coastline. At times we talk for long periods while sometimes we savor great expanses of tightly bonded silence. I felt the weight of my incarceration, the burden of bondage begin to fall away with each new day we strolled together. There were now no days or nights—only the gradual, rhythmic rise and fall of the sun. We never stopped walking; there was no need for rest for we were restful, no need to sleep because consciousness was now transformed into a permanent menagerie of time.

One late afternoon just before the sun began to cast a luscious banded obi over the buffeting sea I discerned the distant, scattered rooftops of a small town in the far distance. It wasn't too long before we neared to discover it was a small, quaint village, bordered to the left of the vertical bands beside it of aquamarine waters and pristine white sand. Its name was Arcombe.

The entire town, its buildings, fixtures, features, streets, rooftops, everything was only of white or red—the crispest, purest radiant white imaginable and a red more true to itself than freshly-let blood. And above it all, like some endless celestial ceiling, the sky was that same red, casting itself like a rippling, enveloping blanket but somehow not blocking the vibrant, scorching sun. The light everywhere was blinding. The town's inhabitants were barefoot, adorned in flowing, long light cotton robes. They were silent, blissful, moving about and going their way without a sound. A tremendous spirit of peace overcame us as we strolled through its narrow outer streets.

I noticed a young boy sitting on a stoop with what looked like an eagle in his lap; a small, sinuous creature with serpentine features was wrapped loosely about its neck. As we walked past him the bird burst suddenly upwards into the sky, circling the courtyard in a manner that framed the hazy white sun above in lazy, broad circles. Its shadow swooped about over the hot cobblestones and played with our toes as we walked on watching this odd but compelling spectacle; we continued to head towards the town's central plaza. All the time the serpent remained gracefully about its neck.

XXXV

I awoke this morning for the first time feeling nothing for Wittgenstein. I have spent countless hours, days, even years addressing his theories. At the very heart of his purported "resolution" of the dilemma of philosophy was the notion that its solution was communicative in nature. Today my world changed; its axis tilted as I realized for the first time the existence and tragedy of his miscalculation.

Where was his heart—his humanity?! His proposed solution to the quagmire of philosophy suddenly seems devoid of any human passion whatsoever—save for the unrelenting veracity of his intellectual argument. Great philosophy, impactful philosophy must include in its genesis the human condition. Whether intentionally or not, Wittgenstein deceived us in the end. He has provided an explanation for the inability of the philosophical *idea* to transcend the restrictions of language—but does philosophy's existence itself require *any* explanation? I have already proposed the idea that "not everything can be explained." Wittgenstein has proposed an "orderly" solution. Was this simply his Teutonic tendency? There are solutions in chaos, and art is often chaotic and at best, imperfect.

XXXVI

In the town of Arcombe a smiling woman in a flowing white dress approached us as we were entering the central plaza and reached her left arm out to take Moon's hand in hers. When their eyes met it was immediately clear to me they had some special bond; there was even a resemblance of sorts between them but I could not discern if they might be friends or even sisters. She turned to walk with us, still holding Moon's hand and leading us in the direction of a large, imposing faded white door that was open and led into an expansive and airy high-ceilinged vestibule, its seating area appointed modestly with several large old leather chairs. It was now high noon. A middle-aged man sat in the center, never looking up at us but clearly sensing our presence. He stared straight ahead with a riveting, unblinking gaze. His eyes were bright green, gleaming, almost molten. His skin was the color of bittersweet chocolate, his hair bright orange and he had large, perfect teeth as white as heaven. Moon's acquaintance explained to us that the man was the highest holder of knowledge and wisdom in the town and that he would speak to us of what he knew that we should know at this time. He eventually began to talk to us in a low, soothing hypnotic monotone. The whole time his eyes never moved or made contact with any of us. I asked him if he was blind but he did not answer and no one else seemed to notice the question.

He began by explaining to us that, as some three thousand years earlier the Greek civilization had reached supreme heights of wisdom and creativity, at this point so much later on mankind should theoretically be enjoying the experience of living in exquisite, almost unimaginable harmony and prosperity. However, it is no secret that this is not the case at all and that in fact, civilization has continued to deteriorate in terms of overall tranquility, natural bounty, cooperation and even civility. He explained to us that this is quite simply because of the inevitable failure of the intellect over human impulse. He referred to the idea of the intellect in its representation by intellectuals—artists, philosophers, writers and so on—and the notion of impulsiveness as being manifested in the extended behavior of the masses in terms of selfishness, sloth and procrastination. He portrayed these ostensibly negative aspects as fundamental and pervasive human qualities, and intellectualism as a nervous habit and expression of gifted people who represent a scant minority of human kind. The true tragedy, he explained, is that our primal instincts and tendencies will always in the end outpower our thoughts—no matter how much those thoughts continue to develop and refine themselves. Desire will trump ideas. Therefore ultimately, philosophy will continue to characterize mankind and society yet never effectively transcend it.

A large woman entered from a side door and presented us with an oval platter of luscious chilled fruits. Our host paid no attention and continued with his dialogue. He explained that we who were gathered here were in a separate place and that one was able to be present in this place if and only if he possessed the ability to live in an absence of desire. This he said was entirely different than a philosophical or religious epiphany or consciousness in that it did not necessarily involve the belief in or role of a solution, Godhead or any dogma. In fact, in our case—whether intentionally or not—our inspiration and reverence was in regard to nature rather than to any divinity.

XXXVII

In my cell that night I struggled one last time to find fundamental truth—and solutions—within the work of Wittgenstein, but found only more flaws:

In order to recognize a symbol by its sign we must observe how it is used with a sense. A sign does not determine a logical form unless it is taken together with its logico-syntactical employment. If a sign is useless, it is meaningless. That is the point of Occam's maxim. (If everything behaves as if a sign had meaning, then it does have meaning.)

Wittgenstein contradicts himself here. Occam either ignored or failed to consider the role of influence upon human behavior relative to the ability of a sign of any sort to effect individual or collective behavior.

In logical syntax the meaning of a sign should never play a role. It must be possible to establish logical syntax without mentioning the meaning of a sign: only the description of expressions may be presupposed. From this observation we turn to Russell's "theory of types." It can be seen that Russell must be wrong, because he had to mention the meaning of signs when establishing the rules for them.

No proposition can make a statement about itself, because a propositional sign cannot be contained in itself (that is the whole of the "theory of types"). The reason why a function cannot be its own argument is that the sign for a function already contains the prototype of its argument, and it cannot contain itself.

This is so, but on the other hand this is the very central crux of Russell's paradox itself.

For let us suppose that the function F(fx) could be its own argument: in that case there would be a proposition F(F(fx)), in which the outer function F and the inner function F must have different meanings, since the inner one has the form O(f(x)) and the outer one has the form Y(O(fx)). Only the letter F is common to the two functions, but the letter by itself signifies nothing. This immediately becomes clear if instead of F(Fu) we write '(do) : F(Ou) · Ou = Fu'. That disposes of Russell's paradox.

This cannot be so: a function can indeed contain itself. It is, to Sartre's argument, of-itself and therefore relevant to itself in that it exists wholly as itself and not necessarily for any other purpose than that it does de facto exist in quod of ipsum. It does not dispose of Russell's paradox—I believe that here Wittgenstein makes a major, egregious blunder: he willingly and knowingly sacrifices the integrity of his argument and in turn his philosophy by using the question of a function being its own argument to attack his loyal supporter and mentor and in a petty manner at that. Russell's earlier attempts upon Cantor's theory regarding the actuality of sets reflected an investigation, or perhaps merely an exploration whereas Wittgenstein's response to Russell was an outright pernicious repudiation. Furthermore, his attack upon Russell was in effect an advance attack on Sartre. Philosophers should not attack each other; they are all in the end performing the same long symphony. But they thrive on this.

The rules of logical syntax must go without saying, once we know how each individual sign signifies. A proposition possesses essential and accidental features. Accidental features are those that result from the particular way in which the propositional sign is produced. Essential features are those without which the proposition could not express its sense.

So what is essential in a proposition is what all propositions that can express the same sense have in common. And similarly, in general, what is essential in a symbol is what all symbols that can serve the same purpose have in common. So one could say that the real name of an object was what all symbols that signified it had in common. Thus, one by one, all kinds of composition would prove to be unessential to a name.

I question the validity of this idea given that a name for an object is itself a symbol and that a singular object can have many different names but that each in an equal fundamental way represent the idea of the object for the common purpose of identity.

Although there is something arbitrary in our notations, this much is not arbitrary—that when we have determined one thing arbitrarily, something else is necessarily the case. (This derives from the essence of notation.)

True, but this is not a fault of language or even simply expression per se; it is merely a characteristic of our expressions through symbolism.

A particular mode of signifying may be unimportant but it is always important that it is a possible mode of signifying. And that is generally so in philosophy: again and again the individual case turns out to be unimportant, but the possibility of each individual case discloses something about the essence of the world.

Definitions are rules for translating from one language into another. Any correct sign-language must be

translatable into any other in accordance with such rules:
it is this that they all have in common.

Languages are only translated into another either for the sake of sharing of information/art, ideas etc. or for the sake of providing explanations to third parties who do not understand the initial language. Therefore Wittgenstein's idea that any "correct" sign language must be translatable in accordance with rules ... is only so within the context of one or both of these two purposes.

What signifies in a symbol is what is common to all the symbols that the rules of logical syntax allow us to substitute for it. For instance, we can express what is common to all notations for truth-functions in the following way: they have in common that, for example, the notation that uses 'Pp (not p)' and 'p C g (p or g)' can be substituted for any of them. (This serves to characterize the way in which something general can be disclosed by the possibility of a specific notation.) Nor does analysis resolve the sign for a complex in an arbitrary way, so that it would have a different resolution every time that it was incorporated in a different proposition.

A proposition determines a place in logical space. The existence of this logical place is guaranteed by the mere existence of the constituents—by the existence of the proposition with a sense. The propositional sign with logical co-ordinates—that is the logical place. In geometry and logic alike a place is a possibility: something can exist in it. A proposition can determine only one place in logical space: nevertheless the whole of logical space must already be given by it. (Otherwise negation, logical sum, logical product, etc., would introduce more and more new elements in co-ordination.) (The logical scaffolding surrounding a picture determines logical space. The force of a proposition reaches through the whole of logical space.)

What he missed here or at least neglected to include is the fact that, based on his suppositions about propositions being able to reach through all of logical space is that propositions are neither spaced-contained nor actually whole in and of themselves as they are not of any dimensionality other than the range of the idea they represent.

A propositional sign, applied and thought out, is a thought.

I am beginning to be disappointed by him, and by those whom exist.

XXXVIII

Today Thalenberg finally stopped by again. I had not seen him for several days. In fact, I had realized earlier this morning that this week was the first week that he also hadn't called or even sent me anything for many days. Clearly he was now beginning to fade away, like all the others. Yet I felt nothing. I didn't need him or anyone else. I had never heard a peep from the firm or my preoccupied boss. Nothing. And again, I didn't care one bit. Ironically, it was at that time that I heard on my small transistor radio in my cell that a verdict had been reached. I had only had to appear twice to testify, and as otherwise the court did not require my presence I declined to attend the rest of the lengthy, tedious trial. But I would have to attend my sentencing.

Penelope Furr was full of life the night she didn't know that she would never go on stage again—she had already given the last performance of her short and ambiguous life. I sat in my cell letting the sound of the radio gradually trickle off into a meaningless, distant strand of garbled monotonous noise. I closed my eyes and pictured the fatal, precarious minutes that occurred just after she'd left the pub. It was one of those scenarios where the alcohol and small talk between she and her two gentleman companions was sufficiently innocuous so as to effectively diffuse the thought of what each of them knew, namely that both men were lustful for her but that all three also knew that nothing would occur. As such she charmed them equally without favor and they responded in kind with clever if unoriginal flirtations and innuendos. The air was nippy and crisp with a fine, subtle mist framing the streetlights and painting the air above with a tranquilizing, pale gamboges scrim. Before very long the superfluous conversation exhausted itself and after her repeated insistences that she was safe to walk the rest of the way to her flat unaccompanied, the other two finally bade their farewells and exited in opposite directions like actors on a stage.

I find the very idea of Penelope Furr enchanting, vivacious, electric. Her luscious, welcoming brown eyes however belied tremendous fundamental insecurities and a conditionality that formed a moat around her ability to express herself ingenuously. Her apartment was small, low-lit, of dark greens and browns that cast an aura within the rooms that evoked the alluring yet threatening tapestry of a forest's edge. Sitting alone in my cell on my last night there I could see all this so vividly. These were the thoughts that were ideas that were facts that were pictures. Whatever else occurred that night within the walls of her home is unimportant; I thought to myself: it doesn't even really matter that she's gone. Everyone is always gone because there could never be a collective arrival of a species.

XXXIX

Wittgenstein went on to address the nature of life in the greater context of the world in which it exists:

The world and life are one. I am my world. (The microcosm.)

There is no such thing as the subject that thinks or entertains ideas. If I wrote a book called The World as I found it, I should have to include a report on my body, and should have to say which parts were subordinate to my will, and which were not, etc., this being a method of isolating the subject, or rather of showing that in an important sense there is no subject; for it alone could not be mentioned in that book.

The subject does not belong to the world: rather, it is a limit of the world. Thus there really is a sense in which philosophy can talk about the self in a non-psychological way. What brings the self into philosophy is the fact that "the world is my world". The philosophical self is not the human being, not the human body, or the human soul,

with which psychology deals, but rather the metaphysical
subject, the limit of the world—not a part of it.

This is the basis of my freedom. I picked up my Eliot
and read:

What might have been is an abstraction
Remaining a perpetual possibility
Only in a world of speculation.

Descend lower, descend only
Into the world of perpetual solitude,
World not world, but that which is not world,

Internal darkness, deprivation
And destitution of all property,
Desiccation of the world of sense,
Evacuation of the world of fancy,
Inoperancy of the world of spirit;

This is the one way, and the other
Is the same, not in movement
But abstention from movement; while the world moves
In appetency, on its metalled ways
Of time past and future.

I am basking in a sea of radiant, burning white light. It is molten yet comforting, enveloping. I see the faces of my loved ones in the bloodied sky above Arcombe, looking down at me without expression.

I have moved from pleasure to anguish to joy to validity. I have learned that the greatest creation is purpose; not life nor art, for they are only but the clay from which we attempt to sculpt meaning—and ultimately fail.

I have returned to my regular constitutional each and every morning which I perform with little or no variance. Immediately below my apartment house the hill into the expansive park introduces a long, straight field penetrated by the periphery of the woods that buffer the neighbourhood from the river below. There I walk inhaling the crisp autumn air, watching people from afar, their dogs and children performing the silent rituals that give rhythm to their lives and espouse continuity within society.

> I soar unto the castions
> And bend to heaven's roar
> Within the ether's moist and lovely belt
> Cushioned by the Alpine air

Soon I shall leave: I will move to Arcombe forever and every day enjoy the sea; I shall perish there free from the inanity, from the fearful and the scaffolds.

We shall not cease from exploration
And the end of all our exploring
Will be to arrive where we started
And know the place for the first time.
We die with the dying:
See, they depart, and we go with them.
I said to my soul, be still, and let the dark come upon you
Which shall be the darkness of God.

We are born with the dead:
See, they return, and bring us with them.

Bibliography/References

Four Quartets, T.S. Eliot, 1944[*]

Tractatus Logico-Philosophicus, Ludwig Josef Johann Wittgenstein, 1921[†]

On Certainty (Über Gewißheit), Ludwig Josef Johann Wittgenstein, from notes, 1950–51

Paradise Lost, John Milton, 1667

The Frederick R. Weisman Art Foundation Collection, Frederick R. Weisman Art Foundation, 2007

Russell's Antinomy ("Bertrand Russell's paradox"), Bertrand Russell, 1901

Jacques Derrida (epigraph), n.d., http://www.quotationspage.com/quotes/Jacques_Derrida

Differance, Jacques Derrida, *Bulletin de la Societe francaise de philosophie*, LXII, No. 3 (July–September, 1968, 73–101)

The Five Habits of Mind, Deborah Meier

A Day at the Races, motion picture, MGM, The Marx Brothers, 1937

L'Être et le néant: Essai d'ontologie phénoménologique, Jean-Paul Charles Aymard Sartre, 1943

Le Diable et le Bon Dieu, Jean-Paul Charles Aymard Sartre, 1951

Saint John the Evangelist, 1504–1506, Piero di Cosimo (Italian, 1461–1521), oil painting on wood panel, 32½×23¼×¼ in. (82.6×59.1×0.6 cm), Honolulu Academy of Arts, gift of the Samuel H. Kress Foundation, 1961 (2989.1)

Le Penseur (originally "The Poet"), Auguste Rodin, sculpture, bronze and marble, 1902

The Magic Mountain (Der Zauberberg), Thomas Mann, 1924

Carmina Burana, Carl Orf, 1935-36

Fantasia on a Hymn Tune by Justin Morgan, Thomas Canning

Symphony No. 8 in E Flat Major, Gustav Mahler

Symphony No. 4 in E Flat Major, Anton Bruckner